Compass North

CATHLEEN ELLIS

Compass North
Copyright © 2019 Cathleen Ellis
www.CathleenEllis.com

Cover design by Launie Parry
Interior design by Brian Schwartz

ISBN: 978-1629671710
Library of Congress Control Number: 2020901406

YOUNG PEOPLE IN LOVE
IN THE HEARTLAND OF AMERICA

OTHER BOOKS BY
CATHLEEN ELLIS

www.CathleenEllis.com

A Scarf of Promise

Old Crooked Road

Castle in the Air

Just Let It Go

Making Our Way

Tend My Flowers

Kara's Love

Together Now

Baskets on Christmas
Lane

Sky Tossed

A Humble Task

Up To Me

What's Beneath

Christmas Bright

Loving Presence

A Voice for Gabby

Shadow to Sunshine

Love Ties

Carry Me On

Roses for Meredith

Future Bright Light

1

"Sarah, ready for me to pour hot cider?"

"10 minutes, please, then call the boys, we'll be all set."

Tyann walked along the fireplace mantle, touching the Mulrenan family pictures Brody showed her through the years. She identified each picture, the year and location.

"I love you, Tyann. I'm just 10 now, and you're 9, but someday I'm gonna marry you. This is my family, and some day it will be your family."

She still heard his boy's voice from that day. She remembered telling him at that fireplace mantle that he was her best friend and that she loved him and wanted to marry him when she grew up. Over the years their feelings did not change, childhood sweethearts, then teen sweethearts. They continued to spend time together, having meals at each other's homes, being in church together at St. Patrick's on Sundays. Tyann helped out at the Mulrenan place in the summer months and especially during the fall corn harvest.

During the evening celebration meal after the completion of the harvest in October 1987 she learned about this Irish

5

family. Brody's dad began as they started in on their dessert of apple crisp.

"Time you knew about us Mulrenan's, Tyann. Sarah and I came to the US in 1970, two almost 18-year-olds. Back in the North (uh, of Ireland) Ryan, my dad, died in a blaze of gunfire in a skirmish with the British army not long before that."

"Brenden, was he IRA?"

"Yes, Ty, he was. I wanted to stay and fight, but pop's Uncle Michael wanted Sarah and me to come to America, get naturalized, take over this property in Iowa, which he deeded to us. Being from the north, I was Protestant, and Sarah, from the south of Ireland, she was Catholic."

He looked across to Sarah and smiled,

"I converted; Uncle Michael thought that best, since dad died, best for Sarah and me, to marry and be united in one faith in a new country. He'd come to America after WWII, bought up property in several other states, property that was in great difficulty. He just couldn't watch over all the land himself."

"He's visiting at Christmas?"

"Right," Brody added.

Tyann came out of her reverie of that time and conversation in October. She found the steaming cider and poured it out. She put the mugs at each person's place. She stepped into the large living room, seeing a fire flickering in the stone fireplace.

She opened the door to the basement family room and spoke out, "Boys, Sarah says it's time."

She heard the clomp clomping of boots as they came up the steps. Tyann waited for Brody; he held out his hand to her. She grasped it. As they walked along she felt the light squeeze of his hand around hers, a gesture she cherished.

She gazed up at him, "Tall, he's so tall, the whole family, trees, Sarah, too. I wonder why he likes me; I'm little and a green-eyed blonde. His hair's so dark and his eyes, why such a piercing dark blue?" she pondered.

The family assembled in the dining room. Brenden and Sarah sat at opposite ends of the table, Brody and her on one side, and Conner, Brody's younger brother, and Uncle Michael, on the other side.

"They look so much alike; genetics crazy in this handsome family, from generation to generation," she decided as she looked around the table.

"Tyann, do the honors, please," Brenden smiled as he asked her.

They all made the sign of the cross, and she began, "Bless us O Lord…"

They signed the cross after she finished and they shared an Amen.

"Delicious, Sarah, you've always been my favorite cook," Michael smiled as he complimented her. The family finished the meal of tender smoked ham, mounds of scalloped potatoes, green salad and lots of warm melt-in-your-mouth rolls everyone pounced on.

Tyann agreed, nodding to Sarah. Sarah gave Tyann a quick wink.

"I love Tyann," Sarah thought, "after all these years, she's cherished by me. And she loves my Brody, how blessed am I. What a grand way to get my girl."

As was the custom, if the girls cooked, the boys cleaned up. Tyann and Sarah fixed plates of pumpkin pie and whipped cream. Everyone returned to the table for pie and coffee.

"So time to share, Brody, my boy-o," Uncle Michael spoke, "your wish, as you mentioned to me, after last corn harvest when I stopped by."

"My wish," he nodded to his uncle," to see Northern Ireland, getting a proper visa for work and study, and using my college money to take a class or two at Milmire Abbey's junior college. My passport's in process, and I've been admitted to the college, oh, provided I graduate from Porttown High."

"Which you will," Brenden emphasized.

"Oh my gosh, Brody, where're you headed?" Tyann shook her head, her eyebrows raised as she gazed at him, "this is the first I've heard."

"Sure, Tyann, my plans're taking shape. Uncle Declan lives in Milmire Abbey, and he's invited me to stay with him during my visit. Milmire Abbey's on the northeast corner of Lough Neagh. The Lough's the largest freshwater lake in the whole of the North of Ireland. I'm staying a school year, getting to know the area, want to see the places of dad's growing up. I'm coming back," he smiled to her, "to begin our life together, to marry you. You've got your senior year to finish, and to decide what you might want to study once we married."

She thought for a moment, thrown off balance by Brody's revelation, "Uh, I'm starting to weigh my options, to make up my mind. For sure I'll be your partner, a corn farmer's wife. That's what I want, my dear sweetheart."

"Same, darlin' Tyann."

The rest of the family cheered for them. After several rousing hands of poker, Brody drove Tyann home.

"So fun to hear your dad and Uncle Michael talking in that thick Irish brogue as we played cards."

"I always enjoy their talks."

"Your parents' American English is really perfect, except when Uncle Michael shows up."

"Right, my parents told me how hard they worked on their American English as they were going through the studying for naturalization, that's when they first got to Iowa."

"They speak, gosh, like California folks, of the West, no accent."

They held hands as they walked up to the Hulfitz front door.

He looked down to her and smiled, "Have a good Christmas, Tyann. You've got aunties coming. You like them so much, so enjoy your family. We'll have New Year's Eve, and the coming spring. I need the time away for a school year in Ireland; it'll be good for us to be apart from each other."

"Happy Christmas, Brody, and I agree I've got a lot of growing up to do; I got pretty reliant on you."

They nodded to each other, hugged and kissed.

She looked up to him, "I love you. I'm happy; Baby Jesus is coming."

"I love you, Tyann, the shelter of your embrace, it's always with me."

ℰ

"Just two days and you graduate; how's that feeling?"

"Great," he smiled to her, "while we have a little free time together, I want to take you to a spot."

He held her hand and they walked away from the Mulrenan farm house. About half way down the lane, he helped her over the wooden fence that bordered the sides of the property to the road. They walked through the pasture to where Tyann saw several maple and oak trees standing. He bent down to show her a wooden stake in the ground. She saw a yellow flag attached to the stake. They walked along, and he showed her another yellow-flagged stake. Before long he showed her the other two stakes. She reached up and held his upper arm as he brought her to the front of the area.

"Tyann, this is my wedding present to you, a home I'll build, with help, for the two of us now, then one day," he smiled and nodded.

She reached her arms up to encircle his neck as he bent down and kissed her. They kissed again and again.

"Pops deeded me a portion of the farm, including this area. He and momma showed me several areas for a home. I picked this one, so lovely with the trees and the fields and fields of corn and soybeans in the back. Once Conner's through school and has his practice established, well, I'll take everything over."

Tyann looked up to him, "Beautiful, such a beautiful area, I love it all, Brody."

"Thanks, I just wanted to make sure. You get to design our home; we'll get started after the next corn crop when I get home from Ireland."

He turned and she turned.

"Facing north, Tyann, our home'll face north, just like you, my compass, facing true north, helping me face true north."

℘

"Dad, I just didn't expect it to be so hard; I miss Brody, and it's only a couple of days. He just graduated, and now he's already in Ireland."

"I know you miss him; but you have your life, and your senior year coming up. It'll be very good for you and him to be apart. And I need your help, my Ty, all summer."

He turned to look at his daughter as they drove home from church, the early service at St. Patrick's.

"Your mom and Mandy, they need their rest, so they'll go to late service. But you and me, we've got the early morning energy."

"Yeah, Dad, to get stuff done, lay it on me, what kind of help?"

"Well, you've mentioned a couple of things to me, stuff I've never paid attention to, but now I am."

"And that's?"

"First, I'm thinking if you want to, I'd step back and have you take over the shop for me, maybe in three years or so. You know so much about the business, helping with the books, continuing to learn how to repair the increasingly complex farm equipment we sell. You're one of my best mechanics, and maybe you might want to take a business class or two at the junior college."

"Wow, Dad, and what else?"

"Our home, you saw how I had the outside painted last month."

"It looks so improved, nice, and we worked together to bring the front and back yards under control. Mom just doesn't have time, or energy, with her 12 hour day shifts at Porttown Manor, and she never gets two days off in a row."

"That's right, your mother works so so hard, medical, it's grueling."

"You, me, and Mandy, when she's not out on the baseball field or running or babysitting, are gonna fix up the inside of our home."

"Nothing's ever been updated, since you bought the place."

"Right, professionals're gonna remove wallpaper from the three rooms that have that, new carpet in all three bedrooms, along with new paint, which we'll do. The same pros're gonna paint our large living, dining, and bathrooms. Mom's getting a new kitchen stove and frig, to match the dishwasher we replaced. Oh, and the cracked kitchen linoleum, and worn rug, your mom and I finally agreed on a wood flooring to replace all that."

සᏖ

"Annie, what'cha think?"

She stood next to her husband, with Tyann and Mandy standing close by.

"It's grand, how bright, cheerful, and clean everything is. You three are miracle workers."

She hugged Tyrone, then hugged Tyann and then Mandy. Annie walked through the updated rooms, marveling at how new everything looked.

"It's our same furniture, but it's so much nicer now."

That day, before their mom's shift ended at 5 p.m., Tyann and Mandy, with Conner's help, returned the furniture back into the living and dining areas.

"Awesome, you guys, your house, uh, it looks way better, what did it?"

"Mostly the new wood flooring, Conner, pros doing painting, removing wallpaper, new carpet and us painting the bedrooms."

"Hard to believe, it just looks so light and bright, and my reward?"

"Yeah, dude, chocolate chip bars, we have a plate, and some you gotta take home to your folks. Don't eat them all now, you'll be sick, a little piggy," Mandy teased him.

"I promise."

Tyann caught his eye as she walked up to him as he got ready to leave. She started to hand him the plate of bars, and then took them back, "Uh, promise what?"

"That I'll save some for my folks."

"OK, hey and thanks for all your help," she said as she hugged Conner.

That night Tyann fixed chicken breasts baked in cream of mushroom soup, rice, salad, and rolls for the occasion of the updating on the family home. She and her sister planned out the meals for two weeks at a time, based on their mom's work schedule.

The family ate hearty, except Tyann. She had a little of everything, her tummy flipping around. She saved some room for ice cream and chocolate chip bars. She decided she had to share, and not just with her dad.

"Everybody, just know I'm sad right now, it's helped to have this project. I miss Brody. But there's something else going on, like my life is making changes that I'm having trouble keeping up with."

"Tell us, my Ty, what changes?"

"My new independence, knowing I can go to work at the shop, and be able to stay all day. I used to go to the Mulrenan's some afternoons helping out, Brody, and his dad and brother. I'm, of course, not doing that any more, not so interested in planning a wedding, 'cause it's a ways off. But I'm anxious to get started in the classes I want to take after my senior year, to help you out, Dad. I'm not exactly sure that's what I want to do, the farm equipment and supply, with my life. Gosh, I've got a lot of decisions to make during my senior year. And Dad, what'll happen if I decide not to be your partner at the shop?"

"My Tyann, remember what I've always told you and your sister, you have to decide what it is that you want for your lives. I can't and I won't dictate that. I'll be disappointed if you decide not to come on board, Tyann, but I can live with it. I'll just have to rethink the next few years."

"Thanks, Dad, and Mom, I hope what we've done the last couple of weeks will make things more pleasant for you when you get home at night. I know how much I like my room, like new."

Tyann stopped and looked from her dad to her mom.

"Mom, I'm concerned about how tired you seem. Working as a CNA is grueling, the hours, the not-so-independent patients, especially the folks with what medical folks are talking about, an affliction called Alzheimer's."

"We both are," Tyrone and Mandy nodded their heads and looked at Annie, "concerned for you," they said in unison.

"Thank you, I think with you girls helping with the night meals, sharing the laundry and housekeeping chores, and outside mowing, that things'll get easier for me." She stopped and looked at Tyann. "That is, until Tyann marries; we'll have to work things out after that."

℘

With just helping out at home, and working at the farm supply dealership Tyann had more time for herself that summer. Her dad suggested she take CPR and First Aid at the junior college. She did, and she liked the classes.

"If something happens at the shop, or out on the farms, I might be able to help someone, even save a life," she told her dad after she completed the classes.

"And mom, well she knows all this stuff; she's so quiet, but she's got a ton of knowledge."

She thought about that and felt a new appreciation for her hard-working mom.

Tyann started getting library books at the Porttown Library on Saturdays. To her pleasant surprise she realized she enjoyed reading as she had when she was little. She hadn't made time in the past few years, just surviving in her reading for her classes at school. Now she read books for pleasure and books about Ireland. The more she read the more concerned she became. People expressed fear, living in Northern Ireland, fear about things that she researched, and found more about.

And every morning she got up and ran, down the county road to the Mulrenan farm, half a mile away. She came to love the running, hearing the early morning birds chirping as she watched the globe of the sun peek over the horizon. The running gave her a chance to think, about some of the experiences Brody might have in Ireland.

Tyann got a letter from Ireland every couple of weeks. Brody stayed busy, liking his summer class at the school, equivalent to junior college in the US. His Uncle Declan kept him occupied with chores around his home and the docks. He was single, a fisherman, but had lots of guy friends, and two ladies who still pursued him. There was no way he would ever marry; Brody would not explain the reason why to Tyann. He wrote the basic same letter to his parents. He wrote a different sort of letter to Conner.

Little brother,

It sure didn't take long for me to see; Uncle Declan, he's so deep into this army. He and his IRA brothers, they've been out, doing planning. It's incredible, the hatred, for the British forces, and between some of the Catholics and some of the Protestants, danger, I feel it. Don't we all believe in the one same GOD? Uncle told me, to say I'm Methodist, if anyone should ask. I've been to his church with him a couple of times, unbelievable how many people know

*him. So, hey, he's way more than just a fisherman. I'll keep you up
to date, as much as I can. I'm pretty positive pops knows what I'm
doing here. I'm not sure he understands how excited and revved up
Uncle Declan is when he comes home from his planning meetings
with his brothers. I've heard the stories of what goes on in Northern
Ireland, since my little kid days, uh, you too, Conner. I don't think
pops discusses any of this with momma, but there is stuff in the
papers and on the nightly news there in America. Keep stuff from
me, this letter and others I'll write, when I have time, in a safe place,
and not a word to Tyann. If she suspects other reasons why I'm
here, she's said not a word to me. Each day's sure an adventure.
Thanks for stepping up and taking over my home and farm chores
and your own, a big load for you 'cause you're an athlete and a good
student. Love, Brody*

 &

"Tyann, you've that free period, and you've got a nice voice,
you should join the school choir," Jenny mentioned to her late
in the summer after they saw a movie together.

Tyann and Jenny Sletery sat next to each other in choir.
She felt a little surprised at how much she enjoyed the
musical effort Jenny suggested. She loved hearing the
blending of voices, soprano, alto, tenor, and baritone. Tyann
always took the hard classes, chem, physics, calculus, and
fourth year Spanish. The difficult work, and the homework,
she always accepted. Now, though, Tyann wondered what
direction her life would take. Some days she hardly thought
about Brody, except to pray for him, between her helping at
the shop, and at home, plus her schoolwork. Her Spanish
teacher kept her supplied with books of Spanish literature
written in Spanish. It was his own personal collection. He
also lent her Spanish tapes to listen to and recite with.

Jenny and Tyann tried to run together on Sundays, before
Jenny's boyfriend came for Sunday dinner. They each drove
their own cars to the running track around the high school
football field.

"Gotta tell you, Jenny, let's run a little slower for a bit, the more I hear and read about Northern Ireland, the more concerned I get. What if we were teens, in Northern Ireland?"

"Ty, you gotta think, that Irish women, must be scared totally out of their minds for their husbands, sons, brothers. It's the bombings, the Irish Republican Army, never knowing when they will strike, or if they're just after the British Army, or if its fighting between the Catholics and Protestants. Will it take until sometime in the 1990's to get this thing under control?"

"I don't know, Jenny, I bet so; I do pray that peace will eventually come. I gotta think though, that the IRA's, they must have money coming in. How do they survive, get the arms they need to keep fighting? All I'm sayin' is that I'm so blessed to live in the US; I can only imagine being a girl up there, the fear."

"Stop, Tyann, let's sit down a minute, somethin' I need to share with you, if you ever tell anyone I'll call you a bold-faced liar, understand?"

Tyann turned to her friend and nodded. They sat next to each other on the grass, near the track.

"My dad, the last year or so, he's let me stay after cards when we and the O'Rooney's have whiskey."

"Yeah, my family's heard about that special whiskey, you drink the stuff?"

"I do take a drink, but I go straight to bed after that. Anyway, after belting down several whiskeys, the talk always turns to their homeland, Northern Ireland, and the anger, it just seems to explode in these guys, my dad and brothers, and the O'Rooney boys and their dad, and once in a while Brody and the Mulrenans, now just his dad and brother, join us, same with them. And Brody's Granddad Mulrenan, he died in fighting the British army. What he wanted, and what all Northern Ireland wants is complete freedom from Britain."

"He died, fighting for freedom, wow, Jenny, like when our country fought for independence from Britain, way so long ago. Our Irish families, sitting here in America, what do they do about their anger that you say just explodes in them when they get to talking at night?"

"Besides praying for their families in Northern Ireland, families here, they contribute."

"Contribute what?"

Jenny watched Tyann's green eyes flame almost to red-brown as Tyann turned to her.

"Get up, let's go, I think you can figure it out, Tyann."

Tyann saw the grim lines of Jenny's unsmiling mouth.

As they started to pick up their running pace, it came to her.

"Jenny, the Ireland families, yours too," she stopped and paused, "IRA, contribute to the IRA. It makes sense, you're all wealthy farmers."

Once she got the words out of her mouth, she felt a chill creeping down her spine. She ran hard.

"That's what Brody's doing, besides going to school and helping out. His Uncle Declan is IRA, just like Brody's granddad was. That's gotta be super exciting for Brody, but there's the danger," she told herself.

She raced ahead of Jenny, wanting to finish the run as quick as she could. She waited for her. As they started to cool down, Tyann looked over to her friend.

"I appreciate what you shared with me. My world just blasted open, so much I gotta think about. Holy crud, where's my head been these past few years?"

"You're in love; you got lots to consider now, Ty."

Tyann stood with her hands on her hips, looking out over the football field.

"Jenny, I stand alone now, and I'm on my own. Hey, and I've just had a serious revelation," she eyed her friend, and shook her head, "Brody's never gonna be happy just being a farmer, after the time he'll have with his Uncle Declan."

They hugged and walked to their cars parked in the lot near the football field.

"I gotta be the best possible daughter that I can be, this last year with my family, help out, talk to mom and dad about any money they've set aside for me, for college. I'm not engaged to Brody; I might want to spend time with another guy. Hey, I have no other experience in dating, none at all, except Brody," she told herself as she parked in the place where her car went, next to the two car garage. "And note to myself, I can never say anything about the IRA, to the Mulrenan's. It's such a part of their Irish history, their loss, Brenden's dad, Brody's granddad."

ℰℭ

During that October corn harvest Tyann only helped at the Mulrenan's part of one weekend. She kept busy in the kitchen assisting Sarah to prepare meals for the hungry harvest crews. One Monday at noon Tyrone pulled his daughter out of school to help repair a corn harvester that stopped working in the middle of a field, during the harvest. The two of them did their troubleshooting, analyzing the mechanical repair that needed to be done. Together they had the machine repaired in a couple of hours.

On the way back to the store her dad turned to her, "My Tyann, we're very lucky to have the parts in stock and for our parts person to deliver the stuff quick to us, right in the field. You and our parts person've both told me several times that we need to keep parts for older equipment. And I appreciate your help so much. You're small, but very strong, which helps in getting into places to do repairs, especially for the emergency today."

"Hey, we just got real lucky on this harvester. Dad, when a farmer doesn't keep his equipment maintained, well this is what happens."

"Right, and I told the farmer he had maybe one more season for the harvester, and then he'll have to get a new machine. Hopefully it won't break down in the middle of cutting next season."

"Oh my gosh, Dad, all that equipment, way so expensive."

"Yeah, we're lucky our farmers have a good relationship with the banks in Porttown, who work with loans for our farmers. And it's also good that farmers share their equipment with neighbors when they can."

ॐ

Father Contran asked Tyann to take over the leadership of the Catholic Youth group at St. Patrick's. When most of them showed up, there were 25 young Catholics, in grades 9-12. Father took the religious training he gave these teens very seriously. And he needed a thoughtful, energetic young person to help him.

"I certainly would be happy to help out for this year, now that harvest's over. I haven't been very good about getting to CY group; this is my final year to have you as my guide, Father."

Tyann convinced Father the importance of pop and snacks after the half hour session and the short meeting the group had three Thursdays evenings a month.

"More will come, if there are snacks, and we can ask for volunteers to bring each week. You'll see, Father, I promise."

With Father's knowing the talks that he would give each week Tyann set a calendar for the group for the rest of 1988 and the spring of 1989. They took a break in the summer.

Tyann liked the results of her efforts with snacks. The group increased in size. By mid-November she and Father had a task for the group. The CY group never helped with a community effort before. And this one involved church members. After Father's lesson, she spoke to the group.

"I'll start, then I'll let Father take over. We have a service request, from the Porttown Knights of Columbus."

"Right, Tyann, some of you may've met the Knowlton couple, in their early 80's, church members for over 50 years. They have no family left here in Porttown. The Knights built them a ramp to their front door, also reframed and installed a wider front door. They've widened door frames and replaced four doors in the home, for the day to come soon when Mrs. Knowlton will need a wheelchair to get around. She uses a walker with great difficulty now. The whole inside of their home needs repainting. It's three bedrooms, a living room, two bathrooms, and a dining room/kitchen combination. All the work's completed, except painting the walls. And the Knights will provide the protective paper floor coverings, paint, rollers, paint tape, pans, brushes, and off white for all rooms. It's the same basic color as now. The walls very much need freshening, many years since painting last occurred. That'll complete the door widening to meet the wheelchair accommodation."

Father saw a hand shoot up in the back of the room. He nodded to the teen.

"It would be our pleasure to help out, Father."

Tyann began to clap her hands; the group got up and clapped their hands. She heard a couple of loud whistles and saw lots of smiles. She helped paint leaders find a Saturday in late November that was a bye week for the Porttown football team. 24 CY group volunteered, 12 for the morning shift, 7-noon, and 12 for the afternoon shift, noon-5, with as many of the morning people who could help returning late in the day to clean up and put furniture from the middle of rooms back in place.

℘

"It's pretty impressive, all these kids, assisting folks who need help," she said to Father as he stopped by at 11:30.

She finished painting the last wall in the master bathroom and then joined the hungry crew who just completed their 5-hour shift. The group coming on at noon just finished their sandwiches and drinks. Leaders assigned the new group to areas of the house that needed finishing up.

Tyann stopped Vanessa, "Tell your folks how much we appreciate the sandwiches and drinks, please."

Vanessa's folks owned a sandwich shop in Porttown, and they were happy to contribute. The entire St. Patrick's parish knew the Knowlton couple and their need. By 5 p.m. most of the 24 reported in to assist in putting everything back in place. The one thing they did not do was rehang pictures. Father suggested the couple might want to do that themselves.

Mr. and Mrs. Knowlton drove up in their car and parked in the driveway. The group stood on the front lawn as the couple, the wife moving slowly with her walker, came up the ramp. They turned; Tyann saw tears in their eyes, as they waved and thanked the young people for their efforts. Father joined the couple. Several teens brought cameras and took pictures. A reporter and camera person from the Porttown paper also took pictures of the group and the couple.

"Wow," Tyann said to the guy standing next to her in the group, "I didn't expect the newspaper."

"Yeah, well this is a big deal, folks helping folks; it's starting to happen more here in Porttown, Iowa. It's a good thing, don't you think?"

"I agree, totally."

Tyann got around to as many of the group as she could, thanking them for their efforts.

"It was so worth it, to see how happy the couple was, once they saw the inside and came back out to thank us," was mostly what Tyann heard as she walked and talked with the group.

She got in her car. Several blocks from the Knowlton home she suddenly felt wrung out, staying all day on that task, with no energy to even keep her foot on the gas pedal. She pulled over to a curb in front of a home and put her head on the steering wheel. After taking a dozen or so deep breaths and letting them out slow-like she raised her head.

"Thank you God, for showing me what service looks like. I've worked with my family on my own home and now this effort. I think what I want to do is help people, somehow help folks; it feels so good to see the smiles on Mr. and Mrs.

Knowlton's faces. There's a sense of appreciation; I could feel that, coming from them."

ဆာ

"How'd you enjoy the Holiday Concert?" she asked as she joined her parents and sister at the kitchen table.

Tyrone brought cups of steaming hot chocolate for all of them.

"Great, you all can really sing, Tyann; it's the first high school holiday concert we've attended," Annie told her daughter.

"Hey, I might decide to join next year, if I have a free period, that matches with the choir time," Mandy nodded to her family.

"Thanks for the hot chocolate, Dad," Tyann spoke up as she smiled to him.

"You gonna tell mom and dad what some of our CY group's doing? It's somethin' you helped set up, Tyann," Mandy nodded to her sister.

"Right, you know about the Christmas boxes St. Pat's does?" Tyann eyed both her parents, "Eight families got picked, folks with really big needs. Father works with church members who share that they need help, or know of someone in our parish who needs help. So each box has individual items requested by a needy family."

"Yes, we know my Ty. What're the kids gonna do?"

"The Women's Altar Society, they've asked the CY group to be the delivery persons for this effort."

"You gonna take the Christmas boxes to these eight families?"

"That's right; Father says it'll be a good experience for us. Hey, so many of us have cars, it'll be a so cool effort."

"Yeah, we'll see how much we have, how little some folks have got, as stuff gets delivered."

"Uh huh Mandy, oh my gosh, Mom and Dad, Mandy and I," she paused as her tears started, "we're so blessed, beyond measure, to have our nice home, enough food to eat, parents who love us and are concerned and thinking ahead to our futures."

She nodded to her parents and grasped hands with her folks. Mandy held their free hands.

Tyrone and Annie smiled to each other and nodded to their daughters.

Annie spoke out, "We are grateful, to you God, for our lives, to be together as a family."

ℰꙩ

"Happy, happy Christmas, Uncle Declan says so also."

"Merry Christmas to you, Brody, and to your uncle, this call, what a surprise."

"This's my Christmas present to you, Tyann."

"To hear your voice, that's the best."

"Thank you for the beautiful Christmas card."

"Oh wow, you got it; I had no idea how long the mail would take."

"Uh, three weeks according to the postmark on the envelope. My fall term class turned out great. We're having Christmas dinner with a woman Declan really likes. She's got a daughter, 16. She and I've done stuff together."

"I'm so glad, Brody; we're not engaged and I think it's great that you have a chance to widen your acquaintances with young women. How will we really know if we're meant for each other, if we don't be with other people?"

"You're right, wow, so good you understand. Have a Happy New Year, and time moves on so quick, won't be long before I'll return to Porttown."

"And Happy New Year to you, Brody, you're in my thoughts and prayers."

"As you are in mine, I love you, Tyann, the light of your loving smile, it's always with me. True north, you're my compass, heading me true north, toward my hopes and dreams, in God's hands."

"I love you, Brody."

She hung up the phone.

"What a wonderful surprise," she touched her hand over her heart, "Love, it goes on and on."

ℰↄ

Tyann checked in with her counselor at Porttown High several weeks after her final semester of high school began.

"Mrs. Frasier, it's starting to come to me that I want to do something else plus be a farmer's wife. You know I've dated one young man, just him, for the last several years."

"Right, isn't he overseas now?"

"In Northern Ireland, living with his Uncle Declan."

"Goodness, that's a dangerous place, his family let him go?"

"Oh yes," Tyann shook her head, her eyes still holding the disbelief she had all these months, of where Brody was.

Her counselor saw the look in her eyes as she winced.

"Please, tell me what you're thinking."

"I gotta talk to my parents to see if they did any planning for college for me. I've worked for the past four years with my dad at his farm equipment business. I do repair work, help with the books and the marketing. But I've never gotten paid for my efforts."

"Good to talk to them, Tyann, you need to let them know what your future thoughts are."

"My mom and I, we talk. She's a CNA, and she suggests that if I'm interested in helping folks, maybe in health care, that I go for a nursing degree, a BSN, and then RN. They get paid lots more money than my mom. She works so hard, but the pay, not so good, and the hours, well, they're awful."

"Your mom knows; her advice to you is absolutely accurate. Tyann, you're getting a very late start on what you want to do. Most students who've applied have already been admitted to their universities for next fall."

"And I've just started making up my mind. Mrs. Frasier, I have a really sinking feeling about the whole money situation; I had a boyfriend for a long time. We planned to marry once he returns from Northern Ireland. I kinda think that my folks assumed I would marry him and become a part of his family, that would be this coming summer or fall. And I hate to say this, but then they wouldn't have to deal with me in a financial way."

"I can hear, your tone, that you're having other thoughts about that whole situation."

"I certainly am," she spoke with a firm voice.

"You must talk to your folks about their ability to help you. As soon as you've done that, you and I, with your parents' help must do a financial aid package, to see if it will be feasible for you to go on with school, if that's what you want."

"I'll do that, and also I applied for a scholarship to Iowa University."

"You haven't heard on that one, have you?"

Tyann shook her head to her counselor.

"What're you thinking of, a career?"

"Nursing, helping folks, like my mom does. She's shared so much about the folks she cares for. I've never really thought all that through, but I'm thinking about it now. My whole life's been so me-centered, just me and my guy, and, of course, corn."

She smiled to Mrs. Frasier, got up and thanked her for her time.

$$\wp$$

Tyann asked her parents to talk to her about money for college. She just put the meatloaf in the oven and poured coffee for her folks and her.

"Mom, your day?"

"Grueling, let's talk about you."

"Tyann, your grandparents, Opa and Oma Hulfitz gave us $2,000 for you and the same amount for Mandy, that was after Mandy was born. It was money for your college educations, or whatever you decided your advanced training would be. We've socked the money away, in certificates of deposit. So the money, it's increased in value a little. And Tyann, you never asked to be paid for working at the shop. I paid you a little for every hour you worked there over the past four years."

Tyann shook her head, "But I helped with the books."

Tyrone touched her hand, "This was my own little separate transaction, just for you, so you never saw it, in any of the bookkeeping."

"I'll be blunt, how much?"

"$3,000."

She smiled to her dad, "Wow, thanks."

Tyann paused, trying to figure out how to ask. She decided to just plunge in.

"Mom and Dad, Mrs. Frazier says we must work on financial aid forms."

"We understand; $4,000 will not pay for your college education. We'll try to help you. But what about Brody?"

"One day at a time; we gotta see how things'll go when he returns to his home. Right now, I'm not sure about anything with him. Our time away from each other's been very revealing for me. When he returns, I'm pretty sure I'll need more time to decide what I really want."

&

Conner and Tyann sat across from each other at the kitchen island in the Hulfitz home. She poured them lemonade, a Hulfitz family favorite in the spring and summer.

"I never see you, Tyann, in school," Conner spoke up after taking a big drink of the lemonade. "This stuff's delicious."

Tyann smiled to him, "Knew you'd like it. Yeah, I know you never see me, glad you stopped by; there's always the shop after school. What's been going on for you?"

"Well, I just got out of track practice. Have you heard from Brody?"

Tyann saw a hint of sadness in his dark blue eyes, "Uh, you're not telling me stuff. And no, I haven't heard from Brody, gosh he'll be back in country before long."

"What I can tell you is that it's crazy, my last note from him, lots going on."

"Yeah, he wrote the same basic thing to me, Connor."

"Please go to Prom with me, Tyann. I've always wanted to go out with you, but I had a brother in my way."

"Way cool," she gave him her wide smile, her green eyes sparkling, "I would like to go with you, our last Prom."

"Were you thinking of going?"

"Yeah, I was going to go, to see all the beautiful young people all dressed up. I certainly am not afraid to go by myself. There're always people who go by themselves."

"Uh huh, me too, I was gonna go alone. And sitting with you, in your kitchen, I just gotta tell you, I've loved you."

She saw his smile to her, and his telling eyes.

He nodded his head, "For as long as my brother's loved you, all these years. I stood in his shadow. But I'm not standing in his shadow now."

An electric shock feeling hit the inside of her head. She paused, swallowing hard, "Conner, you're serious?"

He watched her green eyes flare to a reddish brown, "Yes I am; I know you've always thought of me as Brody's little brother, but you and me, we're the same age."

"And I've always cared about you, just like I care about pops and momma, your folks."

"I've never heard you call them pops and momma, only their names."

"All the Mulrenan's, you're all special to me."

❧

"What a surprise, I didn't know he cared."

"Gosh, Mom, Brody, Conner, me, it's been the three of us, for so much of what's happened the past few years. I've always considered Conner the brother I never had."

"You didn't say anything about that, the brother stuff?"

"No way, I just think it's so special that he's asked me."

"Your dress?" Annie asked as she took the silverware out of the drawer for the dinner table.

"Uh, huh, the dress I wore last year, with Brody, to his Senior Prom. It's a beautiful dress; I'll wear it again and again, to special stuff; it's not just a prom dress."

"That's what you told me last year Tyann, I just admire your no nonsense attitude about clothes, and about your hair and makeup, no fuss, no muss."

Tyann giggled to her mom, a little surprised by her comment. The giggle caught up in her mom and they both began to laugh.

"You are my beautiful daughter, you are."

Tyann felt the tears burn in her eyes, as she hugged her mom.

"I love you, Mom, thank you for my life."

"I love you, Tyann."

❧

Jenny came up to Tyann and Conner as they walked from the dance floor.

"I'm inviting you and Conner to join my guy and me, and my bro and Mandy for card games after the Prom, my house, my folks will have pizza and sodas ready for us."

"Thanks Jenny, that's nice of your folks, a neat end to Prom night. I better call my folks after the dance."

"No need, Mandy already got permission from your mom and dad to come over."

Conner held Tyann close in the slow dance.

"I've wanted to hold you near me for a long long time. After prom's kinda awkward, it's nice of Jenny to include us. It'll be fun."

Tyann looked up into Conner's eyes, "It certainly will be."

The six teens ate and ate, and the game of Hearts went on until they all began to feel weary. Conner drove Tyann home and walked her to her front door.

"Thank you Conner, I had such a good time. You're fun, and funny, and I never realized that."

"This is a special night, one I'll always remember, Tyann."

She stood on tiptoe and he leaned down so she could kiss him on his cheek.

"I care," she smiled to him.

"And I care," he nodded to her.

2

1990

"It's Iowa State, for sure?"

"Yup, for sure, pops and momma been savin' all my life. Ty, what about you, that late start to figure out what you might want to do? Sheesh, I'm forgetting my manners, congratulations to you, our salutatorian, and a scholarship to Iowa, if you decide to go."

"Yeah, but no financial aid for next year, too late, I'm glad I tried, but I'll be with Brody, so stuff's kinda on hold. You still thinkin' Vet School?"

"Uh huh, but that means all A's throughout my four years, undergraduate."

"Right, I know how difficult it is to get into Vet School anywhere, but Conner, you're super smart."

They stood together in the Mulrenan living room. Tyann watched the balloons swaying as guests walked by. And the congratulations banner, she remembered Conner's folks did the same thing for Brody last year. Tyrone and Annie Hulfitz joined Conner and Tyann.

"Congratulations to you, Conner, you all set for, is it Iowa State?"

"ISU, and I am," he nodded to Tyann's folks, "Brody's gotta get back here, so I can go in the fall."

"When's he due in?"

"Next couple of weeks, I know Tyann's getting excited," Conner smiled down to her.

She looked up to Conner and nodded. She smiled to her parents. Inside she felt an icy shield surround her heart. She overheard, listening to Conner, earlier during his graduation reception, as she walked behind them. Conner cut the cake as his dad stood nearby.

"Pops, warning you, Brody's changed."

"I'm sure of that."

As she walked away from them she told herself, "Try to let what you heard go, Tyann, 'course he's changed."

Yet the icy feel did not go away. She thanked Conner and his folks for inviting her and her parents.

A wave of warm relief washed over her as she walked away from the home, like a second home for her for many years, "Dear God, I pray for Brody. You're in charge of him, and of all of us."

℘

Ten days before Conner and Tyann graduated Conner and his folks each got a short note from Brody.

Conner read his note: *"Little brother, I'm headed home, some earlier than I expected. I wrote pops and momma. But you're the only one who knows this. I got shot, a raid. God's thanks, I got away. My wound's a bullet that grazed the side of my head; a scab now, can't even see it. I got lucky I'll arrive unannounced. You got your whole life ahead of you, college, then vet school. I gotta get there to take your place, like you did for me this last year. See you soon. Brody*

ℬ

"Dad, can you give me this afternoon off? Brody's back as of yesterday morning; he wants my help with moving hay bales, plus have dinner with the Mulrenan's, a homecoming meal."

Tyrone smiled as Tyann stood in front of his desk at the supply office, "That's right, you haven't seen him yet. It's quiet; mechanics have it under control. Hey, that's very great he's back. You two can make your plans now. Go, tell him hello and welcome back from all of us."

Tyann's hands shook as she held the wheel, driving out past their home to the Mulrenan's, half a mile down the county road. She parked at the fence that ran along the lane leading to the Mulrenan farm. Cars parked there when they visited the farm. She applied a little light pink lipstick, the only makeup she wore.

After she knocked on the front door, she heard Sarah's voice from inside,

"Come in, in the kitchen."

Tyann stepped into the living room, "Sarah, it's Tyann."

She saw Sarah smiling to her, "My dear boy, Brody, he's got you back, inviting you to help with chores."

"Yeah, which I enjoy doing with him; dad gave me the afternoon off. We were pretty well caught up at the shop, for a Monday."

They hugged. Sarah pointed out the window, "Over there, at the big hay bales, he's taking them down on the loader, moving them closer to the cattle. He's anxious to see you."

"Hey, when did he get in?"

"Really surprised us, showed up yesterday morning, about breakfast time. He didn't want to go to church; we went to late service. He slept all day, 'til dinner, jet lag. We missed you at church; I know you and your dad go early."

Tyann trembled as she walked outside toward where Brody worked. She swallowed hard, her throat dry. She felt her head spinning as she approached. She watched him scoop and load the hay bales on the loader.

"Brody, oh Brody," she shouted over the loader engine.

He turned his head at her voice. She watched his smile as he lifted his hand to wave to her. She heard him shout out, "Tyann, you're here, I love you."

Tyann saw it, a dip in the ground, that Brody didn't see. The skip loader wheels bounced forward into the dip. It threw the loader off balance, the hay bales crashing off the loader and back onto Brody. The whole apparatus tipped to the side. Tyann could not see Brody for the hay and the loader. She heard the scream of the engine. Then there was silence.

She stepped forward, just one step.

"Go, get Sarah, for her to call for help," she commanded.

She ran into the house and found Sarah, taking a load out of the washing machine.

"Sarah, call for help, the police; Brody's buried, under the hay and the loader."

Sarah nodded to Tyann, who nodded back to her.

"We both know; guide us, God," Tyann whispered as she returned outside.

"Don't get close, Sarah, we're not strong enough to move the bales away, wait."

They held on to each other. Sarah kept crying and saying, "My son, God, take care of my son."

Tyann stood, holding Sarah until Conner and Brenden arrived at about the same time as the Sheriff and a deputy. She heard the far-off scream of the ambulance. The next hours played like a movie as Tyann watched the events unfold in the Mulrenan back area. She remembered giving a statement to the deputy, as the only eyewitness to the accident. Everything else seemed to dim once she saw what remained of Brody. She felt helpless, but she did not cry.

As her dad held her hand and moved her back into the Mulrenan home, it circled over and over in her mind, "I must save those I can; I must save those I can."

Sarah made pot after pot of coffee as folks mingled in the home. Tyann moved among the people she loved. Jenny arrived with her mom. They came up to Tyann and hugged her.

She shook her head to Jenny, "Right now, I'm not really here. What's spinning," she pointed to her head, "are the barn dances, all the years of barn dances, that we all attended, right on this property, in the Mulrenan barn. The dancing and the laughter and the smiles, Brody, Conner, you, your brothers, Mandy, we had so much fun, happy times."

"Oh Tyann, what a grand memory you'll have," Jenny hugged her again.

♊

"Dad, I'm talking to God; please just let me go to my room when we get home. Jenny's bringing my car for me and her mom's following. I just can't drive now."

Tyrone looked over to his daughter as they drove back to their home. He touched her shoulder. She turned to him, a wide stare coming from her blank eyes.

"God, watch over her," he prayed as they arrived home.

After Tyann rested for an hour she got up and sat with paper and pencil, writing. It took her 15 minutes to create her list. At the bottom of the page she wrote out what her mind spoke to her earlier, *I must save those I can; I must save those I can.*

Mandy fixed pizza and salad for dinner that night. They ate soon after Annie got home. Her work let her off early to be with her family, grieving for Brody Mulrenan. Conner called a little later to invite them to Brody's graveside service late Thursday morning after a private Catholic mass only for the family. After the graveside there would be a catered celebration of his life at the Mulrenan's.

"Mom and Dad, now that we know about Brody's service, I must talk to you about my future."

Mandy sat in on the discussion because what her family figured out impacted her.

"Sweetie, you're in shock, do you want more time?" her mom touched her arm.

"My wish," Tyann took in a deep breath, "is to start right away at Iowa."

Her parents looked at her. She saw their puzzled blue eyes and furrowed brows, questioning her statement.

"Dad, please come with me. I'm driving to Iowa City on Wednesday, to try for admission to Summer School, which starts next week. Yeah, I know what you're thinking," she nodded, "There's a dorm open for summer school students."

"How many weeks?" Annie asked.

"Ten, if they'll admit me, I'll work my butt off; that'll be my ticket for the fall term. I think it'll help if I show up in person."

"How's that?"

Tyann watched lines wrinkle Mandy's forehead.

She nodded to her sister and smiled, "Because I'll be paying cash for the term; there's no financial aid for summer. I know the school'll like that. But they know I've got an IU scholarship, which will help pay for tuition for every term I make grades, that's starting in the fall."

Tyann called Iowa's admissions the next morning and got an appointment for 10 a.m. on Wednesday. She drove into work and walked into the shop. Her dad had his staff together for a meeting. She did bookkeeping for a little while in the office until her dad came in.

"Got it covered, Tyann, I'll ride along to Iowa City in the morning. I know you'll get in. That's what I just shared with my crew. We're all gonna miss you like crazy. And this bunch, they haven't had much change in quite some time."

"Dad, nobody's indispensable."

He looked at her and shook his head, "I'm having a heck of a time accepting that."

ℬ

Tyann remained silent most of the drive to Iowa City. Her mind kept replaying the years and years of barn dances, with Brody and her friends. She guessed this must be the way she dealt with a death of someone she loved.

"You're somewhere else, Tyann, are you OK?"

"Yeah, Dad, right at this moment shifting ahead, for my future. Hey, no one can go back. But today is precious, don't you think?

"Uh huh."

"And I'm glad I get to spend it with you. We've just really had a special relationship, these past few years."

"That's ending, my Tyann, but I've been blessed to have you in my life."

She looked over to him and smiled as they approached the university, "And I've been blessed, Dad."

Tyrone sat in the Admissions Office waiting room with several other families. Before long Tyann walked toward him. He watched her wide smile and sparkling green eyes.

"I'm in, Dad."

Using the map Admissions gave them they found the summer school dorm where Tyann would live. A student assistant showed Tyann and her dad a room, with a bathroom sink, like the one Tyann would live in. She would share a shower and toilet with three other girls, the bathroom between two rooms. And for the summer her floor remained all female. So far she did not have a roommate.

"You're gonna meet guys and gals," her dad nodded to her as they walked from the dorm to the parking lot.

"I can't imagine I'll have much interest in boys; gosh, Brody, his memory, forever in my heart. This summer it's all about getting started, learning and making grades for admission into the nursing program. And I sure want to try for a job. I won't know about work study until fall, but they're still student jobs that gotta be filled during the summer."

They stopped for lunch before they made the drive home.

"My Tyann, we didn't see the campus, not really."

"It's OK, Dad, 'cause I got the map," she patted it as the waitress brought their lunches. "It's the only way to learn to get around. My counselor got me into three classes, all necessary for nursing."

"You're sure you got time for a job?"

"Uh huh, remember Dad, at home I had seven classes to study for, working for you, plus running the home and cooking. There's not a home here, and I'll eat in the dorm dining room. I'll have plenty of time to study at the library. I'm not even going to attempt to study in the dorm. It'll be too noisy early in the evenings, the only time for studying there will be very early."

Tyrone smiled to his daughter, "Well, heck, we're early birds, you and me."

"So early studying, no problem at all."

She lifted her hand and gave her dad a high five.

℅

The Hulfitz family sat behind Conner, his folks and grandmother at the graveside service. Tyann watched as Michael Mulrenan slipped in to the one empty seat left in the front row. Brody's casket remained closed. Only Tyann, his parents, Conner, and emergency responders saw what remained of Brody at the accident site.

Tyann tried to listen to Father's words, but her mind kept trailing away. "I'm gonna see a whole lot of Brodys in the next few years; but I'll help save so so many folks who God still wants to keep alive for their families on earth."

She drifted over to Conner at the reception, the celebration of Brody's life. Declan called and spoke to his family, Brenden and Michael, the family keeping their thoughts on Brody and all the Mulrenan family. Conner shared that with Tyann.

"Conner, whew, a super tough phone call for your uncle to make, after all the stuff Brody must have gone through, with the IRA, back in Milmire Abbey.'

"Tyann, I shared with my parents, finally, last night."

He touched Tyann's shoulder, as she stood next to him in a dark blue dress, the closest thing she had to black, for mourning Brody.

"Now I'm sharin' with you."

"Spill, Conner, what?"

Conner watched her eyes turn that reddish brown, from their usual green. He spoke in a quiet voice, just above a whisper.

"Brody wrote me, got the letter before he got home. He got shot, in a raid."

Tyann felt a shock of tears as she shook her head, "Unbelievable, Conner, I, well, I always had a kinda dread, about him, about his whole time over there, about what might happen."

"It was a graze on the side of his head. His hair covered the wound by the time he got home, one lucky dude."

"My concern's for you, Conner. How's it gonna work, now that you're going away to school?"

"Nothin's changed right now, Tyann, I'll help this summer. Dad'll hire out; he's gotta have help to get through the corn harvest."

"Everything's changed, in an instant, for me."

"That's right, Tyann," she watched him shake his head, his eyes misting, "man, I need some air."

Conner held her shoulder as they left the living room for the back patio, out onto an area where Tyann viewed beautiful flowers, roses. They stood together, breathing in and out the tangy smells of the nearby roses.

"Ah, your momma's roses, and here's one that we planted for her, Brody and me, gosh, it was a few years back, a peace rose, and it's doing so well."

"Momma's always loved this back area, for sure a place of peace, in her hectic world."

഻

1990 - Summer School
"University of Iowa Alumni Office, this is Tyann."

She listened, taking notes and writing down the caller's name and phone number. She left the message in Norma's mailbox. The staff asked for no interruptions while they were in their offices with clients. Most of the rest of the time they were on their phones.

"Football's just a big deal here at Iowa," Andrea, the acting director of Alumni Services, shared during Tyann's interview for the student position.

Andrea read through her resume and spoke out loud, "Mechanic in the shop, in addition to working in the office, answering phones, and doing bookkeeping, oh my goodness, Tyann, you really did it all. Uh, your shop, where's Porttown?"

Tyann answered Andrea's smile with one of her own, "Dad taught me, I fix lots of equipment, from harvesters, to tractors, to the smaller stuff. And Porttown is right in the middle of Iowa, off 35; we're corn country."

Andrea nodded to her, "You're just the take-charge person we need here. I want to hire you; if it works out, I'd like you to continue during the school year. You'll have some expertise by that time, and with the computer and the IU system. About the phones, we try very hard to have a person talk to each caller to the alumni office; each caller could be a potential donor to the university. I know we all have answering machines, supposed to catch the calls we're not here for. They're a new addition to communications at a person's desk at work. But I personally hate to get a person's answering machine. The other problem is that after people listen to their messages, they don't return calls. It's so frustrating."

"Does the same thing happen with e-mails?"

"That's right, we're just kinda at the beginnings of the e-mail situation. The university is going to an all-university e-mail system. It's been so fragmented with everybody having their own little e-mail setup."

"Uh huh, at my dad's business, he's super strict about answering phones and getting messages to the proper person. He says he's a year or so away from an answering machine, and e-mail, he's not ready for a computer system yet. E-mail delivery is just getting started in our area, over our phone lines. Back to answering machines, a nice thing is that messages that come in after the work day, the calls can be returned."

"Right," Andrea shook her head to Tyann, "if the person getting the message actually decides to call back."

"Sounds like you had a little trouble with that."

"I have, and in a couple of instances, it's cost the alumni office, in monetary and personal ways, for our alumni."

"IU's got a lot of alums."

"Yes, and I wanted you to have this information because calls will start coming in. We have a serious rivalry between a couple of football teams, Iowa and Iowa State."

"I'm writing this down."

"The teams play here in Iowa City this year at Kinnick Stadium on the 22nd of September."

"Got it; I'll find out the time as soon as we know, probably televised, right?"

"Uh huh, but our alums in the area, love to come to the games. I'll get you the schedule for the rest of the football season."

ॐ

"Tyann, it's Conner; I finally called your home and got your dorm room phone number."

"Nice, thanks for calling. You're lucky you got me; I'm going to dinner and then to the library for the rest of the evening."

"Where're you in your summer term?"

"Four weeks to go, home in early August, and back at it after that."

"Tyann, I'm coming to visit you."

"Seriously?"

"That's right, I wanta see you again. You slipped away so fast."

"Yeah, it's helped me, the grieving, being busy helps me put away the sadness. I've got a clear purpose, working, loving my course work, feeling like I'll be able to get into the nursing program."

"Classes?"

"Rhetoric, chemistry, the math class science students take and, hey, I got A's so far."

"You worked super hard in high school."

"Right, this is just the next step. When're you coming?"

"Next Saturday, I got a guest room in the dorm where you're living."

"So you'll spend the night?"

"Right, the next day, come to church with me, my treat for brunch, and then I gotta head back."

"The corn?"

"Doing super, it's gonna be another solid year."

"Everyone does good, if the corn turns out. I'll mail you a campus map, so you can find your way around. Just park anywhere you can find a spot near the dorm. It's the weekend so it's OK to park without a permit."

℘

"I've been to Iowa State five times already. But this is my first time at IU."

"I'm getting used to the place, got my running path, a trail I hike, and I like Father, at the Newman Center, closer to go to church there than away from the university."

"What about the Alumni Center?"

"Like it, wow, this school's got a ton of alums."

"For sure, the best part for you?"

"Talking to the alums, oh the stories they can tell. I've already got a possible tip on someone to talk to about Northern Ireland. I'm just super fascinated by what goes on there."

"Brody, from the grave?"

Conner stopped her as they walked along, touching her upper arm. She saw his blue eyes darken to almost black.

"Right, I hope you're not gonna do somethin' foolish like going to see Uncle Declan."

"Course not, I got my future, the DVM."

She watched as his eyes lightened up as she spoke out, "Solid."

"Yes," he paused and nodded, "I am."

"We've seen most everything on the campus. Want to do an early dinner at a pub we can walk to near campus?"

"Can we get in?"

"Course, just can't have any alcohol, but the burgers are yummy."

"I'm starved, let's do it."

"My treat, OK?"

"OK, but brunch's on me; then I gotta head back."

After they ordered Conner blew out a big breath, "I wanted to make sure you were OK here. I'm impressed by your independence, your being so positive, and clearly, at the medical center, I can feel it, that's where you belong."

"I must save those I can, I must save those I can, Conner, I've said that about a million times in the past few days, since Brody's death. Nursing, it's where I belong. I gotta make the grades, take the classes, and get admitted to the program."

"What about dessert?"

"Yeah, I still got room."

They ordered a brownie, vanilla ice cream over the brownie, with chocolate syrup poured over that, topped with whipped cream, and two spoons.

"Hope you'll date at State."

"Same for you, Tyann, here, there are so many people we will meet, spend time with, maybe date, maybe just be good friends with."

"Like you and me, Conner, good friends, that's what we gotta be, for a long time now. You got eight years ahead, that's a really long time; you can't let anything stop you, slow you down."

"Dig in; I think we'll be full up when we're done with this."

"Yup, we're a couple of little piggies."

"Uh huh."

They walked back to Tyann's dorm, taking their time and skirting a portion of the campus. They parted in the lobby, agreeing to meet in the morning for the walk to mass in the university chapel.

After mass she introduced Conner to Father.

"Tyann's told me a bit about you and your family."

Conner shifted his eyes from Father to Tyann.

"Yes, we've been around each other most of our lives."

Father smiled to both of them, "I understand you're serious about the DVM. I wish you well; study hard. Do you plan to work with vets, starting pretty much now, uh, so you'll know that's what you really want?"

"Yes, Father, I'm sitting in at a vet's office in Ames, starting the Saturday I get there. I'll be immersed from the start."

"Then good luck, Tyann'll keep me up to date on your progress."

Father touched Conner's shoulder, then Tyann's shoulder.

"God bless and keep you, as you travel your paths to your professions."

They walked away from the chapel and headed to Tyann's car.

"Wow, he's pretty tuned in to college kids."

"Yes, he is, a perfect fit for all of us, a positive voice for our futures."

As they sat down with their loaded plates of food at the brunch, Conner asked her, "Will you stay in touch with me, Tyann?"

"I will, it'll be good to have someone familiar to call, as our lives progress. It's gonna be so exciting."

"Maybe we can see each other at Christmas time?"

"For sure, I'll come home for Christmas, until my internship, then who knows."

"That's four years?"

"Right, Conner, wanted to tell you, Brody showed me property where he wanted to build us a home, after he got back from Ireland. Did you know about that?"

"Pops and momma told me, a few days ago. All that's gotta be reworked, now that he's with God."

"Good, I'm glad. I keep you all in my thoughts and prayers."

"My folks, they're struggling, but they see Father Costain and another grief counselor."

"What about you?"

"I've done a couple sessions of counseling, but I'll be gone soon. My bro, his biggest hope for me was to get my education. He's still with me, just like he's still with you, in our hearts. He was doin' what he loved, being in Ireland, and years before that, workin' our land."

She paused for a moment, and then she looked into his eyes.

"I'd like to be your compass north, Conner."

"How's that?"

"Somehow, keep you headed toward your hopes and dreams."

"Keep me headed, compass north, yeah, that makes sense, thank you Tyann, I know I'm gonna have detours on my path to the DVM."

"Yeah, just like my crooked road that I'll have to be a nurse, to save those I can."

He took her hand in his, "In God's hands," he paused, "we are."

They smiled to each other and squeezed hands.

1992 - Spring

He watched her as she wrote down her hours in the ER Volunteer book. It took him back to the first time, his first time seeing her.

"Whew," he stood a few feet from her, "where've I been, that I haven't seen this beautiful little person before?" he asked himself.

She turned and started to put the book back on the top shelf. She went up on tiptoe.

"Let me help you," she heard from the male voice that took the notebook from her and put it on the shelf.

"Hey, thanks, oh to be tall," she smiled to him.

She looked at his nametag and spoke, "Jacob."

He glanced at her nametag, "Happy to help, Tyann," he paused, "what an unusual name."

She kept smiling, "I get that a lot, my dad's name is Tyrone and my mom is Annie. So there you have it."

"You thinkin' about the nursing program?"

"I am, first year, so hoping to be in the program."

"You?"

"Sophomore, starting to look forward to the end of all this, before long, practicums in the fall, and then my internship."

"I can tell you it happens so fast."

"Right."

"You coming on shift?"

"I am; it's great to finish by noon. How long you been on 8-10 Saturdays?"

"Since fall of my first year, I love being here; I stand in and watch trauma as much as I can. I gotta go."

"And I need to start my shift. I'd like to see you again."

"Hey, same here," Tyann smiled and nodded to him.

ଙ

"When're you doing the Ride Along?" Lucia looked over to her as they ran along the path Tyann used since she arrived in Iowa City.

"Emergency Transport's leaving at 1400 tomorrow, for the Med Center in Chicago. That med center's got super expertise, in what's going on with this patient, and they'll be ready for her."

"Turning it around, and back here to IU Med?"

"As fast as we get the patient delivered, I saw a weather forecast, could be a little dicey by late afternoon."

"I worry about you a little, Tyann, classes, the Alum office, ER volunteer Saturday mornings, and then you run, like we're doing now, or hike and head to study. Sunday it's church and you often meet your Little Sister for lunch and time together. Then you study 'til the library closes. Guys just don't get much of your time. Or like tomorrow, along on the helicopter, that's kinda dangerous, don't you think?"

"Hey, Lucia, risk's everywhere. You're right, that's my life, the fellas I see once in a while know that. But it's Jacob who's really turned me on to critical care nursing, with the Ride Along."

ଙ

From the start of her time at IU, Jacob observed Tyann volunteering in the ER at the Med Center. She always asked to watch the happenings in Trauma. Jacob noticed her because he worked a 2-hour volunteer shift right after her, 10-noon. They often bumped into each other as their shifts began and ended. When they didn't, Jacob checked in a Trauma room, seeing her standing back and watching what was going on with that patient and the surrounding Critical Care personnel.

One Saturday that fall he stopped her as she got ready to leave.

"Hey, I see you in trauma observing; you need to know about Ride Along."

After Jacob explained what that process was, Tyann got super excited.

Tyann thought about Jacob as she got ready for her Ride Along coming up in a short while.

"I'm so glad he turned me on to this experience; I'm a sophomore so can really start to understand all the medical procedure, what all goes on," she nodded her head.

She stood near the gurney with the patient all secured and ready for the flight. The care group assembled, a flight nurse, a paramedic, and her, the Ride Along. They exchanged names. Tyann noted their reactions as the med team watched the helicopter land on the roof of the hospital. The intense noise, rushing air, and rotor blades whack whacking once bothered her. But not anymore, she got used to this, a part of critical care nursing, which is what she wanted to do. She observed the young flight nurse.

"Yeah, that'll be me, before much time passes," she told herself.

Once they secured the patient, they all strapped in and spoke to the pilot. He radioed the air traffic tower in Iowa City. Within a short time Tyann felt the powerful copter lift, up, up, into the air. She still felt the exhilaration that captured her mind and body as they moved up and along. She assisted Mia, the flight nurse, in getting vital signs and progress on the patient.

This flight felt calm, easy on her mind, compared to one other she remembered. Their patient needed a fast transfer to an updated facility for specialized care not available at Iowa Med. Tyann felt relieved; this was not someone hovering between life and death from an auto accident. She closed her eyes and thanked God for this special opportunity. Jacob and Conner, the guys, flashed through her mind as she opened her eyes.

"I'm so lucky to have them in my life, a gonna-be nurse and a gonna-be doc, each one of them there for me, helping me along my way."

1992 - Fall Junior year
"I'm so glad to finally meet you, Dr. McGuinness."
She paused for a moment, after she shook his hand, "Are you?"
"I am; I knew that would be your question."
Tyann smiled up to him.
"Please, let's sit down at the table."
He moved books and papers away from them. Tyann sat up, straight and tall, waiting for what he had to say. She directed her gaze on his eyes.
"Martin McGuinness is a very distant family member. And no, I've never met him. I get asked that, especially by students who are into the whole Irish Republican Army conflict in Northern Ireland."
"But you've been over there?"
"Yes, I did a semester sabbatical doing research several years back. I spent a fair bit of time in the north of Ireland. And yes, there was danger; I experienced one bombing, courtesy of the IRA."
He watched worry lines form on Tyann's forehead.
"Share your situation, Tyann."
"I hope and pray that whole Northern Ireland situation can be settled. My special guy from high school, after he graduated, spent a junior college school year in Milmire Abbey, Northern Ireland with his Irish uncle, while I did my senior year in high school. We were to be married after he returned from Ireland. We wrote each other and he called once while he was there. He stayed with family, one an IRA member. My guy saw some IRA activity. He got shot, a graze to the side of his head, shortly before he returned home, in an IRA raid. My feeling is that he super grooved on that military activity; he went for the excitement, but he sure as heck believed in the cause. His family and several other

families with roots in Northern Ireland who live in my area of Iowa are contributors to the IRA effort. The hope and dream of all of them, yeah, that their families and the whole of Northern Ireland'll be free of the British control.

Oh, and what happened to the guy I loved, well, the day after he got home from all that danger, he died in a farm accident. I was the only eyewitness to it," she paused as she shook her head, "unbelievable."

She stopped talking and gathered her thoughts as she again looked at him, "I don't talk much to anyone about this; I'm friends with my guy's brother. He's put his brother's death behind him. I just can't seem to do that, and I've had grief counseling. What do you think, Dr. McGuinness? It just haunts me, the people dying over all this, the danger, in Ireland, even in the train and bus stations in England. The way people're treating each other there," she felt the hot tears misting her eyes.

He watched her for a moment, "The hostilities will continue, but from the folks I know and have talked to, the tension is easing very slightly. There are preliminary talks of stopping the military activities, calming both the IRA and the British army, but that's going to take time. The same can be said for any kind of peace settlement, between the Irish of the North, and the British government. Time, patience, diplomacy, all those things come into play."

"There's no quick fix."

"No, but I have a thought for you. I heard what you just said, no quick fix."

Tyann nodded to him.

"That goes for you, young lady, it's going to take more time for you to move past your guy's death. What's his name?"

"Brody."

"I suspect that Brody floats in and out of your mind, still."

"He does; we were sweethearts from childhood on. He showed me land and had a home staked out for us on this land he owned, that he planned to build for us when he returned from Northern Ireland. Sir, I just can't believe how much that whole Irish situation's affected me. It just pangs my heart when I hear news, of the latest bombing, of the families torn apart, like they're a part of who I am now, having lost a loved one who spent time there."

She watched him nod to her, "It's going to take longer for you; he was a part of your life for many years," he smiled, "and moving on, maybe a young man or two who interest you?"

"Yes, actually there are two," she paused for a short time, "Dr. McGuinness, I'm a third year nursing student. And what I'm learning is the preciousness of each day that God gives us. After Brody died, and implanted in my brain are the words, I must save those I can, I must save those I can."

He smiled to her, "Now, and once you have the degree you will help those you can, I am certain of it. May I ask how did you learn I was interested in Northern Ireland, since I'm a history professor and teach mostly about the Middle East?"

She nodded to him, "I'm a work study, have been for several years, in the Alum Office here at IU. Your name's come up several times, in conversations I've been in and overheard from alums, several former students of yours. Actually I'm kinda amazed at all the info I pick up working in that place," she gave him a smile.

"Interesting."

"Sir, I've taken enough of your time, thank you for your thoughts about Brody."

She stood as he stood. She reached across and shook his hand.

"You've helped me, just to talk it out, and hope for the future for the north of Ireland."

"For you and all the IU students, that's one of the reasons I'm here, to help."

She exited the office and closed his door in a quiet manner. He left it open just a little during their talk. Tyann walked down the hall, passing classroom after classroom and out of the building. She gripped the handrail and stopped for a moment, glancing back to make sure no one was behind her. She breathed in and out, the 10 breaths she always did when she felt like she couldn't take another step. It helped. Tyann looked up into the blue October sky and took the rest of the steps down to the sidewalk.

"God, I hope and pray for better times for all the Irish."

&

"Come home with me for Thanksgiving. I want you to meet my parents and brothers."

"Oh, gosh, Jacob, I need to find out what's going on with my family for that holiday. Dad asked that I help out in the shop, so he and mom could get away for a couple of days; somethin' they've not done, that I can ever remember."

They sat across from each other at their favorite brew pub. Music and talking young people filled the background in Tyann's hearing.

"This is a pleasant change from dorm food, Jacob."

"Glad you're enjoying this; you're a fiend about the studying. I have such a time tearing you away from your routine. It's one of the many things I care about you. You have so much initiative."

"And you're so good for me," she said as she finished the last bite of her hamburger, "more laid back, more patient. You're calm, knowing that everything will fall into place as it's supposed to."

"Hey, Tyann, it's God, I put my faith in Him, that His will carries me on."

"I just have such a hard time putting my trust in Him some of the time," she shook her head to him.

"Hey, always, like on the coin, 'In God we trust.'"

"Are you getting excited about your internship?"

"I am, but I gotta get through my gerontology and public health practicums; they're intense, which you're gonna find out about next semester; the rest of my classes, OK."

"I'll check in with my folks; what do your parents think, about bringing a girl home?"

"They're excited; you're my first. And my brothers, they ask about you. For a while they thought nursing was a girly profession, so they ridiculed me. But now, as I talk about the Ride Alongs and the stuff we see in the ER, they got a new appreciation for nursing care, yeah, on a helicopter, no less."

"Like I always say, my motto, I must save those I can."

Jacob nodded and finished, "I must save those I can."

"Gosh, do I say that too much?"

He took her hand in his, "You can never say that enough, Tyann, it's why we'll do what we're studying to do."

"Dessert?"

"Cheese cake, it's super delicious."

"With strawberries on top?"

"Yeah, and two spoons."

Once they finished the dessert they drank up their decaf coffee.

"That was so good, thanks Jacob."

"Come back with me to my place for a little while."

"No Jacob, you've asked before, and the answer's the same. What I have with you is a caring, comfortable and warm relationship. You've got your internship, coming up soon, and I've three semesters left, uh, two, then the internship. I will do nothing to change or jeopardize what we have together, nothing, not now, not in our futures. Hey, the guy from high school, for me, the one I thought I'd marry; we made a decision to wait for the sexual relationship until after we married. That did not change, even though he went overseas."

"You really do want the best for me," he touched her cheek with the back of his hand.

She gazed into his eyes, "I really do; what's ahead, so intense, for you."

"Hey, you'll still visit me, at home, for Thanksgiving?"

"Gotta check; I'll get back to you."

ℬ

"Whoa, you're not what we expected."

"How's that?" Tyann asked as she looked up, from one Haroldson guy to the next.

The four of them stood in the driveway after Tyann got out of her car and put her bag on the ground. The three brothers exchanged glances and broke into laughter.

"When Jacob told us that you were into trauma, into the air transport stuff, well, we expected."

Tyann broke in, "Some hulking big woman who could outdo any guy medical person."

They all laughed together.

"Not a little bitty beautiful blonde, uh, that's right, ah we're forgetting our manners, I'm Jeff, and this is John, and this is Joe."

They shook hands with Tyann and one grabbed her bag, escorting her into the large farm house. Tyann could see a porch wrap around the entire home. They left her bag near the stairs.

Julie Haroldson came toward Tyann and shook her hand, "Welcome to the Haroldson home. I see you've met J's younger brothers."

"I have, nice welcoming committee, goodness, this must have been interesting for you, raising four young boys."

"It was; still lovin' every second of it, but I had a lot of help; both sets of grandparents live nearby," she smiled and nodded to Tyann. "I'll let Jeff take you up to your room. Come down when you've freshened up for some coffee."

Tyann inhaled the fresh smelling sheets and bedspread as she took several items from her bag and hung them up. She wondered when Jacob would arrive. After she found her way back down and through the large living room, she saw Julie standing near the French doors out into the backyard.

"Pour yourself some coffee; I made up a pot fresh. I expect Jacob soon," she turned to Tyann, "he called earlier from his apartment."

"I think he's getting really excited for his internship to start."

"He is, wanted to tell you, right now, just the two of us. You are super special to him. He shared with me, soon after he met you, about your loss, about being a compass north to your guy. Tyann, you've been that compass north for Jacob. He got sorta lost during the first part of his nursing program. But once he met you, seeing you in ER trauma, then you jumping on the opportunity to get involved in Ride Along, your wanting to be involved in critical care, well, I'm just grateful to you."

She came and hugged Tyann. They stepped back from each other.

"Jacob put up with a lot of not fun teasing, and some pure crap, from his brothers and dad. That's all changed; nursing is tough stuff."

"Yeah, his bros, I'm certainly not what they expected; I told them that," Tyann laughed, as she remembered the reaction of the Haroldson boys as they greeted Tyann as she arrived.

"The guys are out in the barn. Their dad'll be home soon from a meeting in town. You're welcome to check out our home and the grounds outside. Dinner tonight will be lots of soup and sandwiches. Thanksgiving dinner will be at 1 p.m. Both sets of grandparents are coming for the dinner. We potluck lots of meals. This year I don't have to do the pies or the turkey."

"I'd like to help you with other food if I can."

She walked to the kitchen island where Julie stood.

Julie smiled to her, "That'd be great; Jacob didn't mention when you had to get back to your home."

"I'll leave early Friday morning; my folks're taking a weekend away, something they've not done, ever, that I'm aware of. Dad wants me at the shop for Friday afternoon and all day Saturday. Then Sunday they'll come home and I'll head back to school."

"Your dad relies on you, a lot, according to J."

"He does; he was about three years out from taking me on as his partner in the shop, turning over the business to me before long. But, then Brody died. My world changed."

"So a nurse you will be."

"Yeah, my completely different life," Tyann smiled to Julie.

They heard the opening of the front door and a bag drop on the wooden floor.

"Howdy," he smiled to them as he walked toward Julie and Tyann.

"I made it; whew, there was snow, in places."

He hugged Tyann and held her close. He moved around the island to hug his mom. He put his arm on his mom's shoulder. Tyann watched Jacob give her an impish smile, complete with a shine in his eyes. He turned his gaze to Tyann.

"Yeah, I see you survived meeting my bros. Were they decent to you?"

"Uh huh, I guess I wasn't quite what they expected."

"Right, you're small and beautiful."

"My boys, they've come to appreciate the beauty of a woman, a lot," Julie nodded and smiled first to her son and then to Tyann.

Tyann helped Jacob and his mom in the kitchen, preparing for the meal. Jim Haroldson strode in as the family got ready to sit down to dinner.

"I'm Tyann."

She shook his hand and smiled up to him.

"Jim Haroldson, I see you got through the Haroldson boys and their introductions."

Tyann nodded, "Yeah, they say exactly what they mean, for sure."

"Hey, they get that from me."

She heard giggles coming from both Julie and Jacob.

The soup and sandwich dinner turned out to be an experience. Each person made their own sandwich from the piles of meats, cheeses, tomatoes, lettuce and different breads.

Tyann looked from plate to plate seeing the very large sandwiches they all designed. Once they all sat down together and grace got said Julie poured out her specialty potato soup for each of them.

"Mom makes this awesome potato soup with polish kielbasa. And she makes a lot because we eat a lot."

Tyann just smiled to Julie and shook her head.

∞

"Awesome sky tonight, I'm so glad you suggested we get away for a little while. Your family, they're pretty intense. I've got my mom and sister, and my dad, he's super low key, well we all are."

"Uh huh, us Haroldson's, a different bunch, wait'll dinner tomorrow. Hey, the skiff of snow's pretty much gone. I hope that means good travels back home, Tyann."

"I'm only two and a half hours away."

They stopped, gazing up into the light-studded sky, the moon appearing from behind a single cloud.

"Wanted you to be the first to know, I got my first choice, I'll stay at Iowa Med."

They hugged.

"Oh wow, it's what you been hoping and praying for. Congratulations, Jacob, you'll keep your place, still?"

"Yeah, but no more volunteering in the ER, I'm gonna have so much to do, plus there are still a couple classes that we have to attend and participate in. Nursing Leadership should be interesting. It's hard to believe, but pretty much, wherever I go, I'll be in charge, 'cause so much of the staff is aides, LPN's, not that many RN's."

"Especially ones that are BSN's, with the degree."

"You know, within about five years, I could basically be running a program, wow, like a whole orthopedic wing."

"You're right, and Jacob, you know there's the Nurse Practitioner scenario that's coming along, that'll be pretty amazing."

"Uh huh, they write prescriptions and even do small surgeries."

They held hands as they returned home.

"Some incredible things're gonna happen in the field of health care in the next few years."

Before they climbed the stairs to the front porch, Jacob picked her up and kissed her. She kissed him back.

After he put her down, she looked up to him, "Your future, my future, it's gonna be so exciting. I don't think anybody can predict all the ways we'll help folks."

"Yeah, it's a little scary."

"For me, too."

෨

Tyann tried to filter out the conversations and listen to various people talk at the Thanksgiving dinner table.

"So, Tyann, where're you headed in your nursing career?" Granddad Haroldson asked her from across the table.

Everyone quieted down to hear her.

"This coming summer, before my senior year, I'm part of a group getting lots of hands-on in the hospital setting at Iowa Med. I've been doing Ride Alongs on Air Corp Emergency Transports; want to do trauma training so I can be a Flight Nurse on the helicopter flights. So it's my roundabout way of saying, I'll be trauma, critical care nursing, somewhere, someday."

"After I got into the Ride Alongs, I let Tyann know about them. We actually met in the Emergency Room, Saturday mornings, she's done 8-10 as a volunteer; I was follow on 10-noon. That's been for several years now," Jacob smiled as he nodded to Tyann.

"So you two've been in deep, in the medical work, basically since you got into your programs," Jacob's Grandma Merchand spoke up.

Both Jacob and Tyann nodded to her.

"Jacob's mom and I'll keep you all informed about the progress of our two medical folks," Jim Haroldson said.

Tyann heard murmurs of "Yes, please, we want to know," from several family members.

Early the next morning Jacob and Tyann said their goodbyes before she headed out. They drank the hot coffee from the thermos and ate the breakfast rolls Julie set out for them the night before.

"Somehow, somewhere, at Iowa Med we'll see each other again. You're in my thoughts and prayers, Tyann."

"As you are in mine, so much ahead of you, Jacob, good luck and God speed. I'd like to see myself out. I have a real hard time with my emotions when I have to walk away from a loving situation as we have. Please go back to bed and not watch me go."

"You're sure?"

Tyann nodded up to him as they hugged at the front door of the farm house. He kissed her on the top of her head.

"Hold her smile, in your mind and heart," Jacob told himself as he closed the door behind him. He bounded up the steps two at a time. He felt a huge lump in his throat and his eyes misted again as he lay down.

3

Tyann got up and made coffee for her folks. She looked at the kitchen clock to remind her of how long she had left at home. Then her mind rested on Jacob, and the time she spent with him and his family. She remembered, as she gave him her last smile, she saw tears in his eyes. That brought a teary mist to her eyes just now.

"I really miss him, and I think he was sad to see me go. We just got so much ahead of us," she shook her head.

She took the last load of her clothes out of the dryer and added them to her bag. The way she planned it she would have just a half hour with her folks before she would need to drive back to Iowa City. Her parents arrived home at the planned time.

They sat together at the kitchen table as Tyann talked of her visit with the Haroldson family. Tyrone thanked her for watching over the shop.

"I'm just so much more confident with you in charge."

Tyann smiled to him, "You gotta be finding someone else to be confident in."

"Yeah, I know."

"Dad, please, when I come home for Christmas, I want you to have news for me. I've given you my thoughts about who'd be good to replace me."

"You have, and I'm thankful for that, at this Thanksgiving time. Hey, your mom, Mandy, and I missed you, our first Thanksgiving apart."

She looked from parent to parent.

"And I missed you both; you're looking the most rested I've seen you in a very long time."

Annie spoke up, "Oh Tyann, our little time away, it renewed us."

ℬ

"Conner's coming over, this Christmas afternoon. I said it was OK; what are the plans?"

"We're taking wreaths to the graves, then snacks, after our big Christmas meal, and play games. Conner c'n join us in some poker, or other games you decide," Annie spoke up to Tyann. "That boy is always welcome here; been coming over with big brother since he was knee high."

The family headed out to the graveyard after Christmas dinner. Tyann insisted on doing the cleanup so they could go. She knew Conner would be along soon.

She put a Christmas CD on the player and then heard the doorbell ring.

"Merry Christmas, Conner."

"And Merry Christmas to you, Tyann."

They hugged and Conner pulled off his boots. As they stepped away from each other at the front door, Tyann looked up and up at him.

"Yeah, I've grown taller and put on some weight."

"Plus your hair's short; you do look so different, Conner, not sure I'd a recognized you, like passing you on the street."

"Guess I'm getting prepped up for the large animals, Tyann we gotta talk, tell you what's going on."

She took his winter jacket and laid it over a chair.

"Hot chocolate?"

"Sounds super, hey where's your family?"

"Out at the grandparents' graves, with the wreaths they always take on Christmas afternoon. I gotta get to Brody's grave, in the next day or so."

They sat close to each other at the kitchen island after she brought the steaming cups of hot chocolate and set them on the island in front of them.

"Tyann, I've done it, I'm graduating in the spring."

Conner watched her mouth drop and her eyes widen, "What, in just three years?"

"Yup, worked my hind end off, but I've done it."

"Apps in to vet schools?"

"Right, here at Ames, Auburn, and Cornell, Cornell's a long shot; all the programs are good."

"Wow, so you'll be off, working the DVM training, and me, just a snotty-nosed senior, doin' my internship."

"Necessary steps, Tyann, but yeah, we've not gotten to see each other much."

"Yeah, much going on and we each had someone else come into our lives."

"It's over, with the girl. I really liked her, but I had to let her go."

"That's what Jacob and I decided, even though he's at Iowa Med for his internship, so demanding of his time."

"Uh huh, and I know you, every minute of every day, you're occupied."

Tyann nodded to him.

"But now on this Christmas afternoon, I'm free. We could go for a walk along the trail by your place. Uh, what'cha want to do?"

"Let's talk about our programs; I've got the three I'm looking at." He shook his head, "don't know which one might want me."

"And I, I really want to do my internship at St. Augustine's."

"It's a smaller hospital?"

"Right, it's nearby; I'd get to do a lot more hands on, since it takes fewer interns during the spring semester. They've got cardiac, birth care, orthopedics, and cancer."

"Wow, four units, what about surgery?"

"Uh, general surgery, nope, I won't get that, but I'll see surgery through the four units I'd do."

"You'll hear?"

"Middle of next fall semester when hospitals make their decisions for spring semester, for who they want to bring on board, for internships."

"And I'll know," he paused, "different dates for the acceptance letters for the different DVM programs."

Conner noticed her smile grow wider and wider and her eyes sparkle.

"I'm so excited for you, Conner, I am."

He heard the lilt in her voice, and she kept turned to him. He touched her cheek and kissed her, a deep and caressing kiss. She returned his kiss and their tongues teased, touching again and again. She felt the deep burn rise from her groin and move up, and up, way to her throat. They moved their lips away from each other.

"Oh my," Conner shook his head, his velvety eyes wide with desire.

"Oh, my, is right," Tyann looked into his eyes.

"Time, this is what time's done, starting to make us aware of what's going on with us."

He took her hand and held his own over hers.

"We've cared for each other, I, I," Conner shook his head, not able to express what he wanted to say to her.

Tyann took a deep breath and plunged on, "I think all our lives, but this is what adult caring feels like."

"It's shocking, the intensity of desire I feel for you," Conner spoke in a soft voice.

She watched his eyes, the dark blue turning almost black.

"For sure, I've never had these kinds of feelings, so strong, before, and with you, someone I've known since our young days."

Conner pushed his chair a little ways from her as she sat in her chair.

He looked directly into her eyes, "One day, someday, Tyann, you will be the sun of all my mornings, and the fire of all my nights."

She felt hot tears burst from her eyes as she trembled at what he told her. She heard his tone; he meant it.

Just then the sounds of the returning family rang in their ears.

"Hey Conner, we saw your wheels, welcome, and Merry Christmas," Tyrone said as he approached them. Conner stood and shook hands with her dad. Annie and Mandy came and got hugs from him.

"So, which school for you?" Annie asked as they gathered around Conner.

"Whichever DVM program will take me; it would be nice to have a choice. I've been to the other two campuses. Uh, I applied here at ISU. The other two schools are Auburn and Cornell."

"We wish you good luck and hope you'll return to your old homestead once in a while; stop by here and keep us up to date. We don't see a lot of your mom and dad anymore," Annie shook her head as she said that.

"So much's changed, in their lives with both sons gone. I, I don't get home much, 'cause I work a lot at a vet's office in Ames during breaks and on Saturdays, well," he paused, "I'll be there until I start my program. Gosh I've learned so much from him."

Cami watched his wide smile go round to each of them.

"Just like Tyann's observed so much, volunteering her time in the Iowa Med Center ER," Tyrone turned his gaze on his daughter, "learning," he paused, "a bunch."

She felt a soft warm glow wrap around her at her dad's compliment.

"Play games later, and you'll stay for a supper of leftover Christmas, that is, if you've got the time."

"Thanks, Annie, yeah, I don't need to be home until later in the evening. Tyann and I're gonna go for a walk in the snow along the trail at our place. We'll be back."

"Take your time and enjoy each other; your times together, precious," Tyrone gazed first at his daughter and then to Conner. He nodded to them.

⁊

"So beautiful out here, snow blanketing the ground, just enough to still make walking easy."

They started along the trail Brody and Conner established on the Mulrenan land when they were in Scouts. They reached the trees near where the almost frozen brook meandered along. Conner stopped her. She heard the gurgling sound of the water. They turned to each other.

"I'll need to get an apartment, a studio will do, when I find out where I'm headed. What about you, Tyann?"

"In the dorm for fall; in the spring I'm so hoping I'll be at St. A's, such a cool setup there. Years past, the hospital had a nursing program, fairly good sized; catholic hospitals, especially, did a lot of nurse training. My point, the hospital still rents out rooms in what once was a rooming house for nurses in training. It's right next door to the hospital. As a nursing intern I'll be eligible for one of those rooms. So I'd step out of my room and into the hospital, that close. I'll go from a dorm to a rooming house. I'd take my meals at the hospital. They say the food's good there and not expensive. That's my thought for my plan for next year."

"We need to start back; it's cooling off, your plan, you've thought this through."

"And I'm starting to get hungry."

"Me, too."

They laughed together as they remembered the old days where snacks and drinks consumed their thoughts. The Mulrenan's and the Hulfitz's always had cookies, crackers and drinks available, except close to dinnertime.

"Debt, it's gonna be incredible, Tyann, I'll be paying back my vet school loans for at least 10 years after I'm done. Pops and momma can't help me with that, and I don't expect them to 'cause they paid for undergrad."

She hugged him.

"Yeah, I know that's gonna be rough. I don't have that much I have to pay back. I scrimped and saved, worked as much as I could at work study, and my IU scholarship, wow, that's so great, pays my tuition, every semester I make grades, which I've always done. And my folks, they helped me too, so did my grandparents."

"What's your dad gonna do about the farm supply?"

"Hang in there; it's all he's known. He's bought out his silent partner. It's all his now. What about your farm, the corn?"

"Pops'll work it for at least 10 more years and then sell. Uncle Michael's agreed and is starting to divest of some of his properties in other states; he's aging quickly. His dream's pretty fulfilled. Brody helped make that decision."

"Any chance you'll return to the corn?"

"None, except maybe as a large animal vet, in a rural area."

"I want a new life in another part of the country. A lot will depend on my schooling."

ഇ

After an early supper the five of them played poker.

"Like in the old days at the Sletery's," Conner chuckled.

"Except we have German beer instead of Irish whiskey.

Later in the evening Conner and Tyann sat on the floor in front of the glowing fire.

"It'd be great to get back to calling each other. I was bad about that."

"Me, too. But now, the e-mail system is campus wide at IU."

"Same at ISU, yeah, we need to start e-mailing each other. It's a nice way to stay in touch."

They kissed, a slow, tongue-teasing kiss that ignited Tyann's groin. They moved apart in slow fashion. He touched his hand to her cheek.

"I'm on fire for you, Tyann."

She let out a deep breath and nodded, looking into his eyes, "Same."

He helped her up and they went to the front door to put on boots. Tyann pulled on her boots and put on her winter coat as he did. Outside they moved together along the sidewalk to the county road.

"Let's walk for a little."

They held hands and looked up into the overcast sky.

"No stars to see."

"Hidden."

"But they're up there."

He stopped her.

"Time."

"Right, time will help us decide. I love you, Tyann."

"And I love you, Conner."

He picked her up and swung her around.

As he set her down, he kissed her on the top of her head.

"I pray 1993'll be a good year for you."

"I pray that for you also."

$$\wp$$

"I'm in finals, got two the day you graduate, so I won't get to come to your ceremony. I'm so sorry, Conner, 'cause I was so looking forward to seeing you. Love, Tyann"

His e-mail back to her came several days later.

"I'm disappointed that you'll not be at ceremony, 'course I understand. But I got news. Think you know I'm accepted, here at ISU, and at Auburn, decided on Auburn, I know, not what you expected. Time for me to spread wings, to a different place, yeah, Auburn University is in Auburn,

Alabama. That's a haul from here, but I'm excited. I'll be working here for the vet I've been with the last four years, that'll be until a month before vet school starts. He wrote me the most outstanding reference letter, which I'll save for you to read one day. I'm trying for a chance with vets in practice around the Auburn area, to keep doing what I've done with my DVM in Ames. We'll see. Good luck with your critical care unit this summer. It'll help you decide, is trauma what you really want? Love, Conner"

℘

"You've heard what will go on, and we're inviting you to join us. What do ya think?"

"I want to do it; I'll go home in June and help my dad at the shop. Then I'll come back and be a part of the trauma nurse training. I've had a chance to help out in the ER, but just those Saturday hours and I just watched in the trauma unit. And I've done some medical helicopter stuff. This is what I want to do," she nodded to Mrs. Coopville, the IU trauma unit specialist. They sat across from each other at a table in the IU trauma work area.

"It'll be four weeks, all of July."

"Then I'll head home to help out until senior year begins. I'll continue to work on my Spanish. I'm thinking seriously of an assignment out of country."

"Spanish-speaking?"

"I'm thinking so."

"I'll keep my ears open to possible placements."

"Thank you."

℘

Tyann looked around at the students seated in the small classroom. Sixteen students started the trauma training, some of them renewing credentials. She counted, now only six remained, four renewers and two from the student class. In her mind she scrolled through situations she saw and actually helped with during her time in the ER. She knew it was what she wanted, confirming what she felt the first time the ER let her observe in trauma, her freshman year.

"A volunteer, baby steps since then, oh my goodness," she smiled to herself.

The leader walked in, "They want us with the EMT's designated to ambulances for the last eight days, Wednesday-Friday, and then Monday-Friday of your trauma nurse summer course."

"The 11-7 shift, be here tomorrow, Wednesday night, you'll get a chance to see a different sort of world. You got all your paperwork signed off so you can join in, my students?"

"I do have."

"Tyann, you've seen trauma other than the ER and ICU?"

"Yes, Ride Alongs on the medical helicopters IU contracts with."

"What about you, Donovan?"

"Same."

"Either of you ever worked along with the ambulance EMT's?" the leader asked.

Tyann shook her head. She saw Donovan shake his.

"Well, you're gonna be amazed, at the abilities paramedics and emergency folks have."

To herself Tyann thought, "God's gonna be right there with us, His Will, we try to save those we can, but ultimately God decides."

✴

"It's a little bit secretive."

"Oh, yeah?"

"Where the rave will be, kinda spontaneous."

Tyann sat in the back of the ambulance with the emergency personnel. It was 2:45 a.m. Saturday morning, and the 911 call came in just three minutes ago. She listened to the paramedic and watched the EMT's face, devoid of expression.

"Looks like this all night dance party, uh, ended a little early," she heard the EMT.

She felt the jarring bumps as the ambulance moved along on a country road. They were the first of three ambulances dispatched. They headed 3 1/2 miles outside Iowa City, going slow over several potholes.

"My last shift on my last night of this," she told herself.

She felt her stomach spew acid, almost making her want to vomit.

As she climbed out of the ambulance, she heard an occasional "Help me." Her ears searched for more sounds; instead it seemed eerily quiet. Everywhere she saw evidence of an earlier party scene. The shine of the moon revealed bottles, cans, trash, and young people lying in the field. In the background she heard the sirens as the other two ambulances arrived. A triage center went up. The leader went from young person to young person. Very few could stand or walk. Tyann helped carry those unable to walk, but who could still talk. The unresponsive ones went to triage first. Emergency crews counted 26 young people.

She asked the same question of each one with whom she worked.

"Can you tell me what happened?"

"Mighty fine music, dancing, ecstasy, snorted it, then fine whiskey."

Several of them mumbled, "Really know, MDMA, uh, ecstasy, plus alcohol, that shit together's a killer, but awesome feeling, until now."

"I must save those I can," Tyann whispered as she went from patient to patient. "But God, these kids, they told me, the talkers, they knew full well what they were doing."

More ambulances arrived as medical personnel on site made decisions. IU Med could not take them all, so the ones in better shape went to St. A's and one other hospital in the area. Tyann decided she'd never seen so much puke in her life. And she didn't want to see that much ever again.

The land owner showed up.

"Sure as hell didn't realize this could happen. I thought, heck, kids having fun; dancing, the music sounded funky and cool."

Tyann heard him in the background as he stood with the county authorities and one of the medical staff on site. She heaved herself up into the ambulance after two patients got loaded in. Silence and the smell of vomit on clothes filled the air as the ambulance made its way back to Iowa City. Later the crew assembled together before they sat down to chart.

"Thank you, for everything you helped with," the ER leader nodded. "To let you know, she's already been taken away, uh, the one young lady who did not make it. The rest, drug and alcohol-addled brains, well parents and friends will be coming in to claim their kids. One's up in ICU," he shook his head, "too soon to tell."

Tyann went back to her place when her shift ended at 7 a.m. After she cleaned up, she wrote out notes for the paper she had to turn in to complete the summer critical care course. Then she lay down and slept. She awoke four hours later, covered in sweat, from a nightmare about the experience she had out in that field. She showered again and packed her car.

"What's gonna happen to the brains of those kids? I'm so happy to be going home, where there's love, and caring, with people I want to be with; that's the only kinda high I wanta experience."

She repeated that over and over as she drove from Iowa City to Porttown. Silence greeted her as she opened her front door. She brought in her bags and suitcases and put them in her room.

At the kitchen island she saw a note from Mandy, "Lemonade and chippers, enjoy, and welcome home."

She drank the delicious lemonade and ate two chocolate chip bars. She started to feel better as she cleaned up the kitchen island.

"Wow," she spoke out, "I needed to eat."

She surveyed her room and set her belongings from school to the side as she took out clothes to hang up or to wash. Tears shocked her eyes as she fell to her knees beside the bed.

"We're all God's children, all of us. His will for us, what do I do now, after seeing all that horrible stuff not that long ago?"

She lay her arms across the bed and put her head between her arms. She continued to cry for a time, sometimes out loud.

"What now, Tyann?" she asked herself.

She shook her head, "Love myself, love God and my neighbors," she blew out a big breath, "save those I can."

That evening she shared what she could with her family. Her dad held her hand and asked her, "And how does that whole thing make you feel?"

"I'm so sad, so sad, for those young people, for their minds."

One by one, her folks and Mandy hugged her.

4

1993 - Senior Year

"Nuthin' fazes me now," Tyann mentioned to several of her classmates in her Nursing Research class that fall. They also worked together in the gerontology and public health practicums. These friends of Tyann's knew of her summer critical care unit.

In her senior research class she worked with water quality. It's where she decided she wanted to nurse, in locations where medical care had the additional hardship of unclean water.

"We're blessed beyond measure, to have clean water, sanitary facilities, so much we take for granted," she mentioned to Conner in an e-mail to him.

"For the animals, that's the case. If everything's not clean, the animals we treat, they'll not get well. Hey, I sure love what I'm doing, Tyann, I know this's what's meant for me, my reason to be. Love, Conner"

෧

During her nursing leadership care class each student presented a five minute plan for his or her future. Each meeting several students spoke. No one knew when it would be their turn. Lucky for Tyann, her turn came near the end of the term.

"I want to thank Mrs. Lancaster and Dr. Edmond for their efforts," she nodded and smiled to Mrs. Lancaster. "My first position, well, they helped me so much. Two years ago, Angela DeSanto graduated from this program and went to the Dominican Republic, to Punta Cana, a beach community, starting to be visited by folks, especially from Europe. Angela stayed in communication with Mrs. Lancaster. After she'd been at the main private hospital in Punta Cana for 15 months she got a position at the excellent private hospital in the city. She's been in her new hospital setting for six months now. The other hospital had not filled her vacant position. I took my national nurses exam a few weeks ago and am waiting on the results. I applied for Angela's old position. Through a series of phone calls and e-mails, the hospital's decided to offer me the position, contingent on my passport arrival, my nursing test exam results, and completion of my application to work in that country, expatriate status, oh and of course, graduate." She paused and smiled, "I'll have health benefits. But I'll have to sock as much money away as I can from my monthly salary, for my future. I'll be sharing a two bedroom place with Angela in the town, near the hospital. I will speak Spanish as much as I can; the hospital staff there is multilingual; English is the spoken and written scenario among them. But Spanish, it's critical for interaction with patients. Oh, RN's, Angela says, they're in charge, and with my trauma background, I'll see so much of what I've done in my training here. I absolutely want this change of scenery in my life."

"From cornfields to beaches," another student spoke up.

Tyann laughed and nodded her head as she listened to the laughter around her.

∽

Tyrone, Annie, and Mandy stood with Tyann in the hotel lobby. The concierge took several pictures of the family, Tyann in her commencement gown.

Tyann hugged her sister.

"This'll be you soon," she smiled to Mandy.

"Yeah, we'll see."

"Uuummm, you're a sophomore here at IU, not that long."

The family came into a group hug.

"My girls, one day both college grads. could you ever believe it, Annie?"

Annie nodded her head to them, "God's will, and our daughters, they've worked really hard, yes I believe."

Tyann saw pictures in her mind, of the months of her internship at St. A's. She tried to pay attention as the nursing students started lining up, getting ready for ceremony. Scenes rolled out of her head, athletes she assisted in orthopedics. They were her favorite patients. Time and again she repeated, "Up and at 'em, you must walk, and I must stay by your side. We'll keep doin' this and soon after you get home you won't even use your walker anymore. You'll move to a cane, and you'll be heavy duty into physical therapy. Those folks'll take over. They'll help you get back out on that field, or that track, or that court."

As she sat down at the ceremony, babies' faces came to her, the ones she helped take care of, mostly the tiny ones, in the neonatal unit at St. A's. Most little ones made it, but once, while she was in that unit, a baby did not survive its very early arrival. Tyann knew that her job was to bring people seeking health care to being healthy.

"God's will, not ours," she always told herself as she turned her attention to the speaker on the stage above her.

As she walked back to her seat, diploma in hand, she looked out over the audience. She did not see her parents and sister in the mass of faces. But she thought she recognized one face, standing in the back of the great hall where nursing students graduated. She looked again, gave a wide smile and raised her hand a little to acknowledge that she saw him.

"Dear God, it is her, and I think she recognizes me."

Conner asked the Hulfitz family to keep his coming to Tyann's graduation a secret. And they did.

A cake and coffee/punch reception followed the morning ceremony in the hall. The Hulfitz family gathered around Tyann. They came together in a group hug after they found a quiet spot in a corner of the back of the hall. She watched him walk toward the family. What struck her, what she saw, was the light shining in his eyes.

"I love her," his mind blasted out.

"I love him, oh I love him," she whispered out.

They hugged, as he whispered to her, "Congratulations, I'm so proud of you, Tyann."

"Thanks, Conner."

They let go of their hug. Conner shook Tyrone's hand, then hugged Annie and then Mandy.

"How, uh, how," she stopped and shook her head, "did you do this?"

"Ah, Alabama's not that far away, and my semester's completed; I'm back home helping Doc Fletcher here in Porttown for the summer. It'll be an awesome experience for me, right in my own home town.

"That's so great, Conner. You know what's happening to me?"

She felt her face beam hot as she looked up to him and smiled.

"Uh huh, so totally great, that you're doing your dream."

"To save those I can."

He repeated, "To save those I can."

Conner moved and picked Tyann up and swung her around in a small circle.

"I love you."

She heard his whisper, "And I love you," she whispered back to him.

He set her down and kissed her on top of her head.

Tyrone led them to the line for punch and cake. Mandy stepped away and found the coffee area. She took cups of coffee to a round table where they all could sit together.

Tyann swallowed her coffee and let out a deep breath. She closed her eyes, then opened them to see her family smiling to her. Conner covered the hand she placed on the table with his own.

"Ty, glad it's over?"

"Yeah, Dad, you all know how I abhor stuff like this."

"Uh huh, but it's important; we need to celebrate you," Conner spoke up.

Tears shocked Tyann's eyes, "I wasn't there, couldn't be there for Conner, last year, when he graduated," she remembered.

"What's the matter, Ty?" Mandy asked.

"Just hit me again, I wasn't there for you, Conner, on your special day."

He touched her shoulder, "Babe, you couldn't be, you sat in a final, didn't you have two that day?"

"I did."

They were silent as they ate their cake.

Tyann looked around the great hall, seeing the smiling graduates siting with their families.

"And all of you," she gazed from one family member to the other, then to Conner, "thank you so much for coming. This gathering completes my joy, the joy I feel being with you, for accomplishing my long held goal."

A familiar face to Tyann approached the table. Mrs. Elcot touched Tyan's shoulder, "I'm Mrs. Elcot, head of nursing, and I wanted to let you know, family, that I'm so very proud of Tyann. She's spreading her wings, away from us, with taking the position at Punta Cana's largest private hospital. I'm excited for her, and she promises to keep in touch with us." She looked from face to face at the table,

"Congratulations to all of you as I know each of you had a part in helping her on this journey."

Tyann reached up and squeezed Mrs. Elcot's hand. The nursing head moved on to another table.

"She's something, knows all of us nurse grads by first name, where we're from, and what we plan on doing, our next locations."

"Wow."

"Wow is right," she eyed her mom, "and I have every intention of staying in touch with her. E-mail's operational at the hospital where I'll be working."

The family said their goodbyes to Tyann as they left the building.

"I'll be home before dark; my car's all packed and I just have to check out of my room at St. A's. And Conner, I'll see you before I leave, on Monday."

"Good, I work tomorrow 'til Doc wraps up his appointments. We'll talk," he nodded to Tyann. He bent and kissed her cheek, as the family watched.

"You all be safe, getting home, hear?" Conner smiled to all of them.

Tyrone laughed, "And you, Conner, with your heavy foot."

"Yeah, Dad always says the same darn thing."

ഇ

On the drive home Tyann put in her favorite CD which included Martina McBride's *Independence Day*. She played the album again and again.

She nodded her head, "How many times, in the ER, have I seen the abuse. Yeah, this singer, I think, will do more with the whole domestic violence situation. Tyann already missed her little sister, a teen from the Boys and Girls Club, in Iowa City. Jennifer saw abuse as a younger girl, until her mom walked away with her, escaping a psychotic husband. Tyann shook her head, a picture of Jennifer in her mind.

"Switch gears, Ty, they'll be OK," she told herself.

She spoke out, "Jacob, gosh, he told me he had a great first year. I hope I have that kind of report for him and for my nursing supervisor, plus my family, after my first year."

Tyann remembered the last phone conversation she had with him.

"Heed this, Tyann, basics where you're going. The water supply, that's most critical. Don't drink the damn water; you gotta learn bottled, and boiling the stuff at your place. And all your immunizations, I don't want you getting sick. Oh, and I hope you get to do a couple of airlift medical situations, both plane and helicopter."

"Sheesh, Jacob, you sound just like a big brother."

"Hey, Squirt, I've been that to you since I noticed you standing back in trauma, in the ER."

"Like a thousand years ago," Tyann thought as she finished her talk with him.

She arrived to an empty home, a late Saturday afternoon; everyone had to work when they got home that day. Tyann brought in her bags and set them in the hall near her bedroom. She prepared herself for what her mom and Mandy changed in her room. She asked her mom to make her bedroom into a guest room, for folks visiting, which someday, she would do.

"Wow, I like what they did."

The walls of her room, she noticed, were a pale green now, instead of the light lavender she loved. A double bed with a soothing colored bedspread and curtains to match completed the change.

"Hey, there's still plenty of room 'cause they moved out the single bed, desk and little bookcase, "she said as she looked around.

Being a minimalist, Tyann unloaded her three bags, the sum total of everything she now possessed, several of her textbooks, the most important part of her belongings. She worked with Angela, the Punta Cana nurse, with whom she would share a two bedroom place. Angela sent her the short list, of what she would need to bring. In a day she would reload her bags with all clean clothes, including her required nursing uniforms, pink, with short sleeves and loose fitting trousers, that Angela explained she must have. Tyann ordered them and liked the soft pink color. At a fabric store she bought three feet of pink ribbon to match the uniforms. She knew, with the heat and humidity there, that a ponytail, with a ribbon around it, was the best way to wear her long hair. Because of her size, when she tried on her entire outfit and fixed her hair before she left Iowa City, she decided she looked about 15. She asked one of her supervisors what to do about her appearance.

"Your voice, Tyann, use your voice, a louder voice. And when you're speaking Spanish to your patients, talk slow, directly to them, eye contact. It'll take you awhile to get the language inflections. But you'll be amazed, as you hear so much Spanish, it'll become easier to speak it."

Tyann loaded the washer with the first of her loads, then went to the kitchen for lemonade and chippers. Mandy always remembered the goodies Tyann liked.

"Thank you, little sis, we been takin' care of each other since forever, note to self, gotta remember to thank her," Tyann told herself.

She went to the computer area off the kitchen and looked over her e-mail. She saw Conner's note about meeting her at seven p.m. Saturday. He'd furnish the wine and asked her to bring cheese and crackers. And he wrote he had a little somethin' for her and that he hoped Doc wouldn't keep him too late.

℘

Conner drove her back to his family home. They decided to walk out on the property, to find that just right spot to put their blanket down for gazing up at the stars.

"I don't wanta go anywhere. In two days I'll be living in a different world."

"Happy to be right here with you, Ty."

"I brought two wine glasses, thought we'd be fancy."

"Nice, this is a chardonnay, smooth and tasty."

"Well, I've got almost no experience with wine, it's beer at our German house."

Tyann sat, looking up at the sky overhead, as she watched it darken, then shiny specks of light popped out. She shivered. Conner put his sweater over her shoulders. They turned to each other, toasting: Conner, for the enormous learning curve of the first year in vet med school, and Tyann, for completing her degree, her RN designation and getting her excellent scores back from the national exam she took.

"I didn't get more than four hours sleep my whole senior year, with studying, the internship, plus studying for the exams. It's been so super awesome to get seven hours each of the last three nights."

"Yeah, this summer's great; so far I've gone to bed by 10 and gotten up at 5; I'm first getting to the clinic, to see the usual couple of animals kept overnight."

"Like after surgery?"

"Exactly."

They toasted to their futures.

"Your thoughts about Punta Cana?"

She looked into Conner's eyes and began.

"Conner, I want this away experience; it'll help me close on Brody, final healing, my path goes forward. Yeah, per Angela, uh, the nurse I'll be replacing, it's kinda rough duty, three 12 hour days, 6 to 6, but the four days off, (Monday through Thursday) pretty awesome. I work Friday, Saturday and Sunday, I assume part in critical care, back in the good old ER, a lot of action, since it's getting to be a touristy area. It's full pay, 'cause it's 36 hours, plus benefits. I guess what I'll miss most is mass. But Angela says there's a nice chapel in the hospital, and the local priest does a Saturday afternoon service, a 4 p.m. quick sermon and communion. Most of the staff's Catholic, and no one can take more than a half hour for break. So maybe I can catch a part of a mass once in a while.

Angela says some folks from the community enjoy the mass, for the Saturday time, plus it's nice for families visiting their loved ones in the hospital. Hey, I'm committed to two years, to leave the hospital a better place than when I arrived."

"And to save," he smiled to Tyann, as she finished, "those I can. Gosh, hadn't thought about missing a church service. I guess it's just so ingrained in me to attend."

"In me too, Conner, tell me about your next couple of years."

She gazed at him, easy to visualize him with the animals, a gentle big guy with an understanding heart. She remembered how sensitive he was as a kid, when animals at his place got sick or hurt.

"I'll always be with all the critters, big and small, diagnosis, surgery, medications, helping them get well. I've been doing all that in the vet clinics I worked at in my undergraduate time and now with Doc. Unbelievable how much trust the vets I worked with placed in me, still do. So, after third year there's no summer off, no coming home. It's something like 24 units of study/hands-on I've to complete from June until the next May when we graduate."

"Surgery, everything?"

"Yeah, everything, like 19 required units and 5 others to pick from, and big exams to get ready for, like your national nurses test, there's one for vet accreditation."

"That will be some final year, Conner."

Tyann cut more pieces of cheese and laid out more crackers.

"This all tastes so wonderful."

"Yeah, Conner, it's being outside, in this woodsy setting, seeing the trees ahead, the sky above, and hearing the little brook that still flows down by the trees.

They sipped most of their second glasses of wine and finished the snacks.

She smiled to him, "Oh, and being with you, Conner."

For just a moment her mind flitted back to the short time she and Brody spent back away from where she and Conner sat. They spoke of a home, building a home together.

"Let it go, let it go," she nodded to herself as she shut the thought from her mind.

"You were with Brody, just then."

She smiled to him and nodded, "You flat can read my mind."

"Not always, but I saw you wince as you shut the thought out of your head."

"Oh Conner, in God's heart, there's no one like you."

They turned to each other. Longing flooded Tyann, her groin area heated to almost explosion. She looked into his eyes, dark, intense, desiring her. He took her hand and lowered it to his erect penis, straining through his old jeans.

"So much desire," he whispered as his breathing quickened. His hand moved under her bra and his finger circled her hardened nipple. She felt her vagina swim with fluid, wanting him, aching for him. They stood and undressed each other. He covered her with his big body, stroking her back and as she stroked his. They knelt, her breasts pressed against him and his penis moving against her tummy. They kissed and kissed, each kiss leading to the next, their tongues touching as they pressed closer together.

Tyann's head snapped back, away from his kisses. She looked up into his blue-black eyes and put her head against his chest.

"I can't, not now."

"I know, my beautiful one."

"There're our tomorrows."

"Two years, decisions."

They clung together. They helped each other with getting dressed.

"Warmer now?"

"Yeah, oh Conner, so much livin' to do."

"And loving you."

They stood together, looking up at the darkened sky. He handed her a small box, "A little somethin'."

"I don't have anything for you, Conner."

She watched Conner pat his hand over his heart.

"Oh, yeah, you do, your love, memories, right here. Here, let me help you."

She held up the small gold necklace with a tiny heart in the middle.

"Oh, thank you. Would you help me with it?"

She turned. He clasped the piece. It fit snug against her neck.

She moved around to face him, "My love for you, is always, each day," she paused, "and I pray for you."

"As I will pray for you."

They grasped hands together and squeezed, "In God's hands."

"Yes."

They agreed to say goodbye as Conner let her off on the sidewalk in front of her home. Tyann sat on her front step, trying to compose herself. She kept sobbing. Conner pulled over on the side of the road about half way home. He gave up trying to control his tears and just let his sadness take hold of him.

5

1994 - Punta Cana

"Too many have infections, the patients, they've picked up while they've been here."

"Didn't come in with the infection?"

"Yes."

How long's this been going on?"

"Noticed it, about six weeks ago," Dr. Schlitz nodded to her. "It's not getting any better."

Tyann left the nurses station and went to the housekeeping storage area for the floor (including the ER area) on which she worked. She knew exactly what to do. From there she approached the housekeeping/maintenance staff. They nodded when she asked if they could help. For her third task she drew water samples from five different faucets on the floor and from faucets in the kitchen and laundry areas. The med techs ran water quality tests. Over several days she assisted the housekeeping staff who worked the 7-3, and 3-11 shifts.

They all wore masks the first time she introduced the new procedure.

"Bleach, you must use bleach; our supply folks've ordered odorless bleach. But we have to use up the smelly bleach we have first."

"Why bleach?" a housekeeping person inquired.

Tyann went on to explain that only bleach killed many of the bacteria, invisible but ever present everywhere in the hospital. She talked about the infection increase that occurred after patients were admitted. Most of the time the illness they came in for got treated. But these bacteria, new to patients, it was making some of them sicker than when they entered the hospital.

The housekeeping staff understood. She showed them how everything had to be wiped down, the beds and everything else in the room, door knobs, besides floors, walls, and all equipment within the room, things not thought about. Bacteria infested surfaces. Once she worked with them she started in with the nursing staff and doctors, about the absolute necessity of washing hands, after every patient, after every procedure, even after gloves got pulled off. Most never thought about doing that before. But they figured it out, because patients got sicker, not better. Housekeepers brought in boxes of gloves, for every room where patients got treated.

"Glove up," became the mantra for everyone. The maintenance staff installed antiseptic wash containers outside every room holding patients, and in many places throughout the floor. All staff, everyone, saw the constant reminder about clean hands, and masks for staff who came in sick themselves.

"Pretty grim, when staff get sick, don't know how to handle that," she spoke to the doctor in charge of the hospital.

"Fact of life, we gotta have staff, to make this hospital a place where sick folks can come."

"Got it, short staffing is worse than having someone come in who's got the sniffles."

Over the next few months, from May to November, a staff member on Tyann's floor kept statistics on the patients and their illnesses. After four months of the new procedure, patient health improved. Tyann saw it, as did the rest of the staff. The bleach plan went on throughout the hospital, for all patients. The laundry and kitchen also worked with the hospital administration, improving the water quality in washing everything used in the hospital. Especially important was water use in the hospital kitchen to wash fruits and vegetables for cooking and baking.

ॐ

Thanksgiving Day Tyann invited two nurses and two doctors who were not on shift for a dinner, to celebrate that American holiday. She planned to bake a chicken in a pan with chicken broth, peeled and quartered potatoes, canned onions and carrots, using the small apartment oven. She asked each guest to share a dish or drink they loved, from their own country or state. One guest was German, a doctor.

Garrett Solmiger, the German doctor on staff, asked Tyann out soon after she got to the hospital. She declined, told him she had to get a handle on her life, that she still grieved for the guy she planned to marry back home, a guy she saw die, right in front of her eyes. And he had a brother, someone else she cared for a lot.

Tyann got the nerve to ask him to this Thanksgiving dinner. And he accepted.

"You excited me from the first time I saw you, someone who looked so Germanic, the blonde blue eyes, and you are," he nodded to her after he accepted her invitation.

The Swedish doctor and the Icelandic nurse each brought a favorite dessert. The nurse from Alaska brought salad, and Garrett brought two bottles of a white German wine, to celebrate the occasion.

Tyann gazed around at her guests. They sat crowded together at the circle table after standing for Tyann's grace which four of them knew, since childhood. Tyann handed them serving plates of food. She asked Jenny to put a little of each food on her plate.

"Please, everyone eat. For seconds, just get up and help yourself."

She placed the serving dishes on a table near where they ate. Tyann took in a deep breath. The whole apartment smelled of the onions and carrots baked in with the chicken.

"Uuummm, this is delicious," Ian Rolde smiled to Tyann. "Where'd you learn to cook like this?"

Tyann explained her mom's work situation, that she cooked, helping out since she was 10.

"Yes, everything's wonderful," several others commented.

Everyone shared clean up chores. They decided to wait for the tasty desserts. Garrett poured more wine for those who could have it. A guest would leave before long to get ready for her 12 hour shift starting at 11 p.m. After the special pie and cheese cake, the guest headed out. And serious poker began.

"Thanks for bringing the poker chips, Jennifer."

"Yeah, like you, Tyann, my family and others in our small Alaskan community played a lot of cards."

They finished off the second bottle of wine after two hours of poker. Jennifer got most of the chips. The four of them decided they needed to play again, if they could ever coordinate their shifts.

"It's been so great to get away and spend time together, so fun," Ian and Jennifer agreed as they left at the same time.

"Thank you for all this," Garrett came up to Tyann after her guests left.

She nodded as she looked up to him.

"I miss my family, back home in Iowa. You all are my family now."

He moved closer and closer to her. He bent down as he caressed her lips with his. She returned his kiss with a soft kiss for him. He kissed her cheek and then gathered her into his arms. They held together for a time.

"That feels," she paused, "so wonderful, your hug, Garrett."

They stepped back from each other.

"I want to spend time with you, on the beach or visiting in town, a dinner out. The hotel developers're putting up some large resorts. You know, I have a car; let's go exploring, you and me."

"My hours, working Fridays through Sundays, the nice thing is, when I actually get off at 6, I have the rest of the evening, and all day Monday through Thursday."

"Except I know, dear one, that you volunteer at the free clinic downtown on Wednesdays."

"I didn't know anyone knew about that."

"They love you there, Tyann, you are a superior nurse. Actually I learned that from a priest who also helps out. Father says a mass at the hospital chapel, volunteers, and does counseling."

"Wow."

"Happy Thanksgiving, it's a great way to give thanks for all we have, you Americans really demonstrate that."

She saw a bright light in his sky blue eyes as he looked down to her. She walked him out, smiled and nodded to him. He walked several steps away, then turned and waved to her. She raised her arm to him.

Tyann finished putting away the dishes and cookware from the dinner. She wanted everything in order when Angela got home from her 3-11 shift.

"Oh my gosh, I didn't even ask him. I wonder if he volunteers at the free clinic?"

She got her answer after she talked with him.

"I do volunteer at the clinic, on Fridays."

"That's so helpful, for the sick people," she smiled and nodded to him, "So many who don't have any way to even get to the clinic."

"And when they do, there're often in pretty bad condition."

"My goodness, and when we send folks on their way, well, we all contribute to a fund so they can ride the bus, at least part way home."

80

They swam, then talked some more, apart and then near each other. They stayed closer to shore, swimming and being aware of the rip tide, since they were all alone. Garrett and Tyann sat on a large towel, spread out on the beach, a soft sand area he discovered exploring when he first got to Punta Cana. She watched the late afternoon sun keep disappearing as clouds sped along above where they sat. The breeze they felt dried them off without so much as a towel.

"It's still quiet at the hospital; I guess residents want to celebrate Christmas and the New Year here kinda like in America. They don't want to come, want to be with family."

"Have noticed, many tourists here, the hotels are full."

"Yeah, people escaping the cold winter of Europe."

"Here, I promised you wine."

He opened the bottle and poured the wine in the paper cups Tyann brought.

"And I also wanted us to have cheese, and crackers. I still have trouble remembering, no raw fruits or vegetables, yuk, trouble keeping my mouth closed, not taking in the sea water."

She heard the soothing sound of water lapping on the beach. They sat together, sipping the wine, enjoying the sharp taste of the cheese, and looking out over the water glistening in the early evening sun.

"This place is a paradise."

"It is. And I'm so happy to spend this time with you."

"What will happen to you, Garrett?"

"I'll doctor at the hospital until September. There'll be a replacement; a fair number of medical people who want to come here, on special assignment. I'll return to Stuttgart, to resume my practice. My father plans to reduce his hours, so I'll pick up some of his patients plus mine, a busy family practice."

"How in the world could he let you go, I mean, come to Punta Cana?"

"Yeah, he did something similar during his early years of being a doctor. He wanted me to have a similar experience. Except this place, Punta Cana, is quite exceptional. He didn't have this beach kind of opportunity. And I don't have the kind of debt to repay for medical school, as the doctors do in America."

"Right, young American doctors cannot do this; you're very lucky."

"I'd say blessed; it's what you say a lot to me, you say that I'm blessed beyond measure to have this opportunity, to practice, to use my Spanish, and still set money aside for my future."

She nodded to him, "Which's just exactly what I'm doing. I want this adventure in my life. I wanted what Brody got, time away from his country and family. Except he welcomed the danger, the fighting, skirmishes, the IRA with the British army. But I hate danger; I just want to help folks, like we're doing. I'll take all that I learn here back with me."

"What about your guy?"

"Time, Garrett, that's what we chose to give each other. His whole being's focused on making the critters better, improving their health care," she paused, "well, just like what we do with humans. We're only e-mailing every few weeks. He understands my situation, as I understand his. What about you, is there someone special you'll be returning to?"

"I heard back at Christmas. She married a doctor, and they live outside Berlin."

Tyann saw sadness film over his eyes as he held her gaze.

"Ouch, at the holidays, I'm so sorry; the same thing could happen to me, he might meet a fellow vet student who lights up his world."

"He could," he paused, "how do you Americans say it, if you can't be with the one you love, love the one you're with."

Tyann looked out over the waves and thought, "Is that the way it is, I wonder?"

For a time they sipped their wine and ate more cheese. The wine kept Tyann's mind fuzzy and warm. She leaned her head on his shoulder as they sat together.

"And us, you and me, where do we go from here?"

He turned to her.

"Oh, Garrett, I care for you as I do all the staff; we're a team, pulling each other along to help folks get well. I want to spend time with you, if you'd like to."

"Yes, I want to. When I look at you, your hair and eyes, your beauty, reminds me of Germany, of all the young people there. Gazing at you makes me homesick, homesick for my homeland. I'm falling in love with you, I am. I can't help it, your dedication, how much you care for the patients."

She raised her lips to his. They lay together after they undressed each other. Tyann felt herself exploding from wanting him so much.

"I've never," she whispered.

"I'll help you."

Gently and slowly he eased himself into her. She felt enormous stretching as he moved back and forth inside her. The overwhelming ache she felt for him began to subside as he murmured her name. Semen spilled out over her vaginal area as he withdrew from her. They held each other close, on their sides. They kissed again and again, and she let him check her.

"You bled a little, but to be expected. Let me clean you."

After he did, he suggested they go for a swim before they left the beach.

They faced each other in the water.

"I was scared, Garrett, but you made it so gentle."

"After you heal, I hope you'll enjoy intercourse more and more. Uh, I was being a doctor just now."

They laughed and held on close, as they tread water together in the deeper area. Her wine buzz continued later as he hugged her and walked her to the door of her apartment.

"Thank you for this afternoon and evening."

He looked down to her and gave her a gentle kiss on top of her head.

ᛉ

She stood, ready for work, drinking coffee in the kitchen.

"This is what is, this is my life, today. What the hell did I do to myself yesterday?" She started to cry, then stopped and whispered, "Tyann, you're an idiot, no condom, is he HIV or AIDS, or has STD's? For the love of heaven, we're medical people, that was so frikin' reckless."

Her mind flashed back to the beautiful beach, with a fine, tall man. The remembrance of that man got replaced, that moment, by a vision of a tall, muscular man wearing cowboy boots, blue jeans, and a long sleeve plaid shirt. He smiled, and a light of love shown in his eyes. He stood, waiting for her.

She walked to the hospital that morning, still cool outside. Mid-morning she took her break and went outdoors with her coffee. The patio had umbrella-covered tables and comfortable chairs. In one corner she heard a small waterfall gurgling recycled water. A statue of the Blessed Virgin stood nearby. She walked toward Mary.

"Mary, oh Mary, I pray that single intercourse does not bring a baby. Mary, I resolve that I cannot drink wine anymore. The same thing almost happened the last time Conner and I were together. I may have alcoholic tendencies, not able to handle the stuff. Please help me watch myself. I need my friends now; I'm so disgusted with me."

She finished her prayer, touched the top of Mary's head, and stepped away from the statue.

When she got to her nurses station, she said a second silent prayer, "God, what will be, for my life, in the future, is up to You, guide me."

$\mathcal{E}\mathcal{O}$

Garrett asked Tyann out once after their date at the beach.

"Thanks, but no, you understand that I've someone."

He heard the kindness in her voice and saw her understanding eyes. He got it.

At a small farewell party before he left in September, he asked to talk to her. They stood together in the back of the meeting room that doubled as a celebration area.

"Thank you for helping our patients; wherever you go when you return to the states, well, they'll be lucky to have you."

"I feel the same about your patients, in your family practice, back in your homeland. They'll be very lucky to have you. God bless you, Garrett."

She reached up and hugged him. He held her close and kissed the top of her head.

$\mathcal{E}\mathcal{O}$

"End of May, it's been a year for you, Tyann; what will next year bring?"

Ian, Ilsa, Jenny, and Tyann sat together on the tiny back patio behind Tyann's first floor apartment. The four of them became good friends, trying to be together at least once a week, since they all worked days.

"More of the same, I hope, Ilsa. I know I will lose all of you. By October I'll be the last one remaining on this special assignment for the hospital."

"There'll be new, excited medical folks for you to work with," Ian mentioned. "You'll welcome them, and you'll become good friends, just like what's happened with us."

Tyann's excellent work continued to be noted by the doctors and administrators at the hospital.

හ

"Golly, Tyann, just responding back to your e-mail about you going on 6 p.m. to 6 a.m., F-S. That's gonna be way different. Congrats on your great ratings, you're an awesome nurse, so caring! Before you know it, you'll be back in the good old US of A, it's November now, just to the end of May, '96. And wow, I'll be in my final year, starting then, no break, one year to the DVM. I'm really looking forward to all I'll learn in the special units, and the ones required. Happy Thanksgiving, and I'm getting so excited to see you, not long now. Love, Conner."

Patients flocked in. Tyann's hospital was overwhelmed, as was the hospital where Angela worked. The public hospital in town had to close its doors after hordes of sick people stormed the emergency area.

Christmas Day came; the crisis continued. Sick people lay in beds and on the floors through all the hospitals. In most cases, only a sheet lay beneath the person. Emergency antibiotics came by way of air military transport.

The medical staff rotated through, catching a few hours of sleep when they could. They all had the typhoid shots. Staff who did not keep themselves well hydrated and fed started to get sick.

Santa Domingo provided microbiology and water treatment staff for Punta Cana. The government scientists pointed the diagnosis as typhoid. They searched and found the source of the contaminated water, and also food the water contaminated. At the end of the first week in January, the officials found the contamination source, a seepage from an old mine that corroded pipes in the main water supply for the city of Punta Cana, including all the hospitals. An engineering firm changed out the eighth of a mile of corroded pipe.

As Tyann and all the staff began to see, typhoid appeared to have a wallop. After two weeks on antibiotics folks began to feel better. But soon after that, some typhoid patients got sick for a second time, some requiring hospitalization.

Tyann's body walked through a haze, sleeping four or five hours when she got home after 6 a.m. and then going in, still groggy and sleep deprived, after that, for the three months of the epidemic.

"I feel like I'm back in school," she shared with other staff, "except that I'm with sick people all the time."

By now she had complete responsibility for the ER, which for weeks mainly held sick folks, not trauma victims. On Valentine's Day, she got to finally be the critical care nurse, on a flight to Santa Domingo's top private hospital with a brain cancer patient. That night she slept in an air-conditioned hotel room, and in the morning she met her helicopter crew for breakfast in the hotel dining room.

She looked from the pilot to the EMT and shook her head.

"I checked in with the nurses station. Our patient died in the night. We tried guys."

"He went to God," the pilot whispered.

She squeezed his hand, then the hand of the EMT who assisted her on the flight.

She saw tears in the pilot's eyes, "I'm so sorry, your first one?"

"Si, uh yes, it is."

The three of them said the *Lord's Prayer*, in Spanish.

When she arrived back from Santa Domingo, she learned that three nursing staff at the public hospital succumbed to typhoid.

"Who can we spare?" the chief of staff at her private hospital asked her. "We must help each other, the medical staffs, we must."

Tyann worked out a schedule with the head nurses on several other floors. Two other nurses and Tyann each took one night shift a week at the public hospital, leaving the staff on their floors to cover. After three weeks of assisting, the crisis of short staffing appeared to be waning. The typhoid patients trickled in, to all of the hospitals in the area. Some folks died, never coming into a medical facility from home.

A normalcy returned to the lives of the people in the Punta Cana community. The strict adherence to the bleach process continued at the hospital with Tyann doing an occasional monitoring. Tyann became friends with a new doctor and a new nurse on staff. They worked together through the typhoid crisis. Peter Schonen, the new doc from the Netherlands, started to have symptoms of the illness. He received his protection from typhoid, but at times it showed up anyway. He ended up with a very mild case. Maria, the new nurse from Italy, and Tyann checked on him at his apartment, making sure he took in enough liquids.

"I'm just so weak; why me," he complained to both of them as his condition improved.

"Stop whining," Maria told him, "you're such a guy, but you are even a lousier patient than most."

"Sorry, I've never really been sick before, and I hate it. I understand now about what sick feels like, I mean being really sick," he shared with Tyann and Maria when he got clearance to return to work, part time, until the chief of staff OK'd him.

℘

"I read your short message; I'm so sorry about the epidemic, Tyann. Remember how you and me, we talked about water quality. I know God's in charge; that's helped me with my concern for you, no word since before Christmas. While I was home for the holidays, I stopped by your folks. They're worried real bad for you, 'cause no word, no e-mail or Christmas card. I tried to assure them that you'd had all your shots, that you're protected.

It won't be long and you'll be back. I love you. Conner"

She talked it out with Peter and Maria at their last time sharing before Tyann went back to the states.

"Give yourselves, uh, it's been two years, apart the whole time, you and your guy?"

Peter gazed at her after the three of them shared dinner and beers at Maria's place.

"Yup, two years apart."

"Get employed; you gotta keep sockin' away any you can, for your later life, plus for living now. Where's he located?"

"Auburn University, Auburn, Alabama."

"Big town?"

"Not that big, 60K plus, the university's a huge deal there. I'll do contract stuff with visiting nurses, going into homes to check on sick folks. I know I can't get into the hospitals or clinics 'cause, well, Conner'll have four a year; all specialized units; a bunch of them he has to have to graduate with the DVM. After that, God's will, the two of us maybe will move on to a practice for him."

"Do you care where you'll go?"

"Nope, this, this time with you all, Punta Cana, a kind of paradise, this's been my adventure for my life, my by-myself adventure. The ocean, the sand, the beach, the warm climate, oh my gosh, the sunsets, but most of all medical care, all aspects of it, I got such an education here. When I first started nursing school my pledge was to save those I can, save those I can. It'll always be at the forefront of my thinking, making it personal, save those I, emphasis, I, can."

In March Tyann returned to communicating again with her dad and mom. She let them know the crisis was past. She applied for her nursing license in Alabama. And she planned to do contract visiting nurse work, finding a studio apartment in a small community on the outskirts of Auburn. Conner's critical fourth year, they would not have much time to spend together. So much changed within Tyann, she shared that with her parents.

She went back on days, still F-S in the ER 6 a.m. to 6 p.m., for the final months of her time in Punta Cana. She started to get acquainted with two local police officers, who often accompanied an ambulance, or they brought in someone with difficulties: stab and bullet wounds, facial lacerations and concussions. One afternoon the three of them chatted after the patient stabilized, and they finished up the paperwork.

"You mentioned the wonderful dances of the folks who live here."

"Yeah, I'd like to learn one of those dances before I leave."

To Tyann's delight, Carlo invited her to go dancing with his friend and his friend's girl at a disco downtown.

Tyann smiled and smiled, enjoying every second.

"Yeah, young thing, you're getting into the swing of the dance."

Tyann danced with him for nearly three hours; he had a strong lead and she learned the dance she wanted to take back with her.

He moved next to her and let her do the dance moves.

"You'll be a great teacher for your man. What's his name?"

"Conner."

At the end of the evening, Carlo walked her to her door.

They spoke in Spanish, as they had part of the evening.

She switched to English, "I hope there's a girl out there, looking for you, Carlo."

"Maybe," he paused, "but I will miss coming in to the ER, to see your blonde and blue-eyed beauty. It's been such a pleasure getting to know you, Tyann, such a lovely name. I consider you an angel, sent from God, to help people improve their health."

"Thank you, good night Carlo."

She watched him take her hand, bow to her and kiss her hand.

"Good night."

After she got inside it hit her.

"Oh my goodness, he's an angel, protects us also, and I didn't get to tell him that," she spoke out.

She did get to tell him, on the next to last shift she worked. The damage to the young man's abdomen and heart from the knife wounds doomed him. Carlo knew the boy.

When Tyann shared his death with his partner and him, Carlo broke down. Tyann pulled him from the busy nurses station into a trauma unit not being used. He broke down and cried.

"His mamma needed him; he quit school and was working to help put food on the table for his five younger brothers and sisters."

"God's will, Carlo."

He looked Tyann in the eyes as she nodded to him, "You're an angel, sent from God to watch over us. Continue to be that angel, we need you, Carlo."

She hugged him, and he hugged her back.

"Ready?"

He nodded to her after he blew his nose and wiped his eyes.

They walked back to the nurses station together.

"Thank you," he tried to smile to her as he and his partner left the ER.

6

1996 – Return to the United States

"You look wonderful, my Tyann, so tan, and your hair's lightened in that sunlight," her dad smiled to her.

They hugged.

"Your flights?"

"Good, it'll be so wonderful to be home. I got kinda homesick for the States, but I had responsibilities."

They stood at baggage and claimed her three bags.

"My gosh, this all?"

"Yup, I brought home less than I went with, but these are still the same bags. I shipped a picture of a beach painting. It's my memory of Punta Cana. The best gift I got, my Spanish. I know it'll help me with my nursing here."

"We got the painting; very glad it didn't have glass. You mentioned that.

We didn't open it."

Tyann rested on the trip from the airport to Porttown. When they arrived home, Tyann saw her trusty wheels sitting in the spot where she'd always parked it.

"My car, uh, I thought Mandy took it over."

Her dad helped her take her bags to her room.

"Mandy bought a car; she wanted you to have your car back. We'll go in and get the title transferred back to you. I'm paying your first six months of car insurance and your new license plates, course you'll have to make all the changes once you get settled."

"Gosh, Dad, that's wonderful, for you and mom to help me like that."

"Gotta help you get transferred back. I know you'll have to get private health insurance 'cause your nurse position is temp, and doesn't cover health."

"I'll be home until Sunday morning. Then I gotta make the trek to Auburn. I start my position on the next Saturday."

They sat together at the kitchen island.

"Lemonade and chocolate chip bars, oh Dad, you all remembered."

"Actually, Mandy made the bars, and I've learned how to fix up the lemonade."

Tyann looked around at the family kitchen.

"Gosh, this kitchen, luxurious, a nice-sized stove, compared to the living situation I had. To have clean water, air conditioning, those are things I so took for granted before Punta Cana, but not anymore. We Americans possess so much," she paused, "Dad?"

"What's that?"

"Mandy, sheesh, bought a car, how can she afford?" she paused.

"Yeah, she left IU after last semester; not happy, not satisfied with her major, or with her surroundings."

She shook her head to her dad.

"She's assistant manager at a grocery store in town, and she got her own place. She's got some debt from school, no scholarship, like you had."

"Happy?"

"Yeah, she seems to be; she has a gift for handling people, the employees and also the customers. She's been allowed to make some changes and fire a couple of less than satisfactory employees. The store's appearance is much improved. She's got PR and marketing skills."

Tyann smiled to her dad, "Hey, she gets that from you, just listening to dinner conversations over the years, she's picked up a ton of info. She's always been our listener."

They settled in and each had a second chipper.

"So you guys are empty nesters, how's it feel?"

"Very hard for us, we love you and your sister so much. But we gave you roots."

"And wings, Dad, and wings to fly away as we needed to."

"You'll be proud of your mom; she's a supervisor at her nursing facility. She got some online and practical training. One of the medical people there saw the promise she has. Now she doesn't have to work all the time with patients, and the facility runs on eight hour shifts, like some hospitals, 7-3, 3-11, and 11-7. She's making better money than before."

"Dad, tell me about you, after two years."

"My second in command's doing well; I think you may have been a 9th grader when he graduated. Anyway, he's trained up like I trained you, straight out of high school and he's gotten married and has a baby. He'll be a fine man to take over in six years or so. He's smart, committed to stay, wants Porttown to be his home for a long time now."

"Retire then?"

"Probably never retire, but I'll maybe drive tractor, or some other piece of equipment I always worked on. I'll want to do volunteer work, like you've always done. Did you volunteer in Punta Cana?"

"Yeah, at a free clinic for the many with nothing, in the community and surrounding clinic, usually on Wednesdays. There were several of us from our hospital who gave their time."

"Conner?"

"Into his first of 20 some units of special study he'll have to do between now and graduation next May. Plus, he's like me, there'll be an exam he's gonna study for, to get his accreditation."

"It'll be a surefire way to practice what he's learned from the books."

"That's right, hey, thanks for driving me; I got so much to do."

"Go to it; I'll head for the shop. Your mom and I're gonna take you out to dinner, welcome home, and wishing you good luck in your next assignment. Mandy'll try to join us; depends on close up."

෴

Tyann met Sadie, her property management person, at the appointed time to get her keys to her apartment. She waited for Tyann to check out the small place, and sign off on changes that needed to be corrected. The central air conditioning unit for her place did not work. So Sadie would take care of that.

"Yeah, please have the repairman your management firm uses come in and fix it. I'll deal with phone and internet situation. He's got a key, right?"

"Correct."

The apartment didn't meet her strict cleanliness standards. Tyann worked a couple hours on the bathroom and tiny kitchen. Her new mattress and new carpeting met with her satisfaction. She thought back on the crude living situation.

"If I have guests, I want this to be nice."

She remembered the two years of living in a different country.

"I'm really, really glad to be back," she remembered saying that to Sadie when she got the keys.

A day later her phone got installed.

"Marvelous and quick technology," she told her phone man. She mentioned to him what service was like in the country she had been in.

ℰℭ

"Oh wow, Conner, you're home."

"So good to hear your voice, Tyann; you got your phone, that's good."

"Yup, I'm all settled in, except for internet setup. Glad I'm minimalist, 'cause this place is tiny. And the air conditioning got fixed. Actually it's really cold for me, after all those months of heat and humidity. I often just keep windows open, until late in the day."

"Tyann," she heard him stop talking and a sob came from his throat.

"Conner, tell me."

"I gotta step back, from you, from our relationship for a little while. I got so anxious to see you, well, I was at the end of my first unit; I almost botched a simple surgery. I gotta repeat the unit before they let me go on. I'm sorry, I'm not thinking straight, can't keep messing up. I won't graduate with my class if I don't get it together."

He tried to clear his throat, but she heard his tears through his voice.

"Concentrate on what you're doing, Conner. I understand that as a medical person myself. We can wait to see each other. We have our whole lives ahead."

"When's your assignment start?"

"Saturday."

"Think it'll be interesting?"

"Yeah, I'll help improve lives here. Some cases where I was, the folks, beyond hope when they arrived at our door."

"I'm sorry."

"I gained a real appreciation for health care in our country. But we still have a ways to go, especially in rural areas, in the South and in big cities."

"Thanks for your call; let me get through this do-over unit, and the next one I'm assigned to. I'll call you. And to let you know, 'cause I know you'll ask, yes, I'm studying for my accreditation, besides everything else going on. I love you, Tyann."

"And I love you, Conner, as you've always been, you're in my thoughts and prayers."

At 2 a.m. Tyann still couldn't sleep. She got up and fixed coffee.

"It's kinda nice, I don't have to be so quiet, now that I live alone," she spoke out. She stepped out to her small first floor patio. It faced out on a greenbelt area. Her tears began, "So disappointed, but I had to come back to some place, and I guess this is a good place. I have a job and a home. Stop the pity party, Tyann. God blesses me, beyond measure."

She came back in and lay in bed.

"Have a little gratitude, my goodness."

She slept then.

ॐ

Tyann accomplished the training she needed to do for beginning her visiting nurse duties. She worked Monday-Thursday, and alternated Saturdays and Sundays. She serviced a number of patients, all in the same Auburn area.

After a month she and her supervisor spoke about her progress with patients.

"Tyann, I want to thank you, for your special service to three of your patients."

They sat together in a corner booth of a small café, in the same area of town where she had patients. They drank iced coffee.

"How's that, Mrs. Martin?"

"Fans, you're brought each of the three a fan."

"Oh, that," she eyed her supervisor and shook her head, "No central air conditioning, so they needed a fan for their bedrooms, for sleeping."

"Also, you have a way, with the families of patients. You've pointed out quite a few hazards that other nurses either didn't notice, or didn't report. And the families are grateful, things they didn't pay attention to either. It's that you always put it in terms of yourself and your family, like 'if this was my grandma, I would remove those small rugs, 'cause sometime she might trip and fall over one.'

And night lights, the patients themselves, and their families, just didn't realize what a difference having a small light on, can help, in the middle of the night."

"That's from childhood; my parents had night lights in the hall and in the bathrooms, for if we got up in the night."

They shared several other aspects of her training and then Tyann left for her next patient. It surprised Tyann at how she enjoyed moving about, not enclosed in a particular area or hospital, but free to be out and about, enjoying the weather of the day.

Ben D. became one of her favorite visits. He lived in a lovely home, kept up by a housekeeper who came in several times a week. He had two hover-children, who called him daily to see how he was getting along since his wife died of cancer the year before. His phone calls to his children became more positive.

"My Tyann, that's what I call my lovely visiting nurse, oh she's beautiful. She's got me up and about, instead of sitting all day. We even go for walks outside with my walker. If I do real good and my doc approves, I'll be able to walk outside by myself. Won't that be something?"

His son and daughter approved, and told him to keep up the good work. They also let the visiting nurse supervisor for their dad know of his improvement. They felt Tyann should get the credit for helping their dad. They mentioned that Tyann did little niceties for their dad, while nurse and patient were together. He began dictating letters to her which she wrote out and mailed. He got reconnected with several old friends with whom he'd been out of touch. Before long his doc indicated he got on well enough to just have the housekeeper come. His medical situation had improved enough to stop having the visiting nurse.

"That's always my goal, to make you stronger, to go on, by yourself," she spoke to Ben D. on her last visit.

"I will miss you, my beautiful angel."

She saw tears stand in his eyes after he said that.

"You take good care of yourself. You're in God's hands."

He nodded to her, "I must always remember God."

They hugged and she turned and waved to him before she walked out of his front door.

Tyann couldn't help herself as she walked to her car. Her tears came, "What a nice man," she nodded to herself.

∽

Communication stopped between Conner and Tyann, no e-mails or phone calls. That occurred in July. The only situation Tyann could envision was difficulties with some of the units he had to pass. She remembered that they saw each other twice, once for dinner at his place, and steaks she cooked out on the small grill at her apartment patio.

She tried to hike several trails in the area at least once a week. Now she wasn't on her feet all day long hiking became pleasurable, and she met someone on a weekend hike. They seemed to start the trail at about the same time on the Sundays when Tyann didn't do nursing.

She hiked fast, and once passed him, then slowed down and hiked next to him.

"You hike this trail a lot?" she asked.

"I do, Sundays, after mass."

"I knew I'd seen you somewhere before. You go to early mass."

"I do, and I've certainly noticed you at church; you're a beauty. You just look so different with your ponytail pulled through your IU hat. It's so different from church."

"Yup, hey, I'm Tyann.

"Lucas."

They shook hands as they hiked along together on the widening trail.

"Say your name again."

"Tyann, yeah, my dad's Tyrone and mom's Annie, so my name."

"Nice name, never heard it before."

For a few weeks, until nearly Thanksgiving, they met and hiked that same trail together.

"Never talked much with anyone in the medical area, you're fascinating; all the technology coming on board in the field, ultrasounds, the MRI situation, CAT scans, wow."

"But your field, exploding, with something called the Internet."

"Uh huh, it's been around for a while, government kinda got it going. At Auburn, we can't keep up with the computer upgrades, the storage systems. I'm an IT guy, but it's kinda overwhelming. I graduated in Computer Science from Georgia Tech, but whoah, it's a whole new world of connecting people, e-mail, that's just the beginning, who knows, one day, oh I can't even imagine."

They continued up the last few minutes to the top of the ridge.

"Here's where I connect best, out with nature, breathing the air, the smell of the pines, and it's sure nice to be with you."

"I like being with you," she turned to him and smiled, "and I'm getting used to the mountains, actually tall hills. From Iowa cornfields, I went to Dominican Republic beaches. So I have a beachy feel for everything. What I like most right here is the clear, sweet air, still a tiny humid, but nice."

"Just gonna ask, are you dating anyone?"

They sat down beside each other on a long rock and pulled out their water and trail mix.

"Sure, had a long term, long distance relationship with a man who was in my life since childhood. Right now, we're not seeing each other. We're giving ourselves more space. But I haven't dated anyone since I moved here in late May from Punta Cana. She paused, "Wanta share?"

"Kinda same, long distance, but did say our goodbyes nearly a year ago.

It's a bitch to break up during the holidays."

"Yuk, that's for sure."

"I'll always love her, Tyann, but it wasn't gonna be a relationship that would work. There's gotta be love, but also liking the person as a friend."

"Wow, that's for sure; I really gotta examine that, the friendship part."

"Your guy?"

"Yeah, seriously pressured, senior in the DVM program at Auburn, and he's got so much training, called units, to do, a year, from last May through this coming May, until graduation."

"Sounds like you two've made the correct decision, to step away. Hey, you've got your career to carry on."

"Uh huh, the visiting nurse situation is temporary, no benefits, I gotta decide where I really want to be. I thought I'd be a follow on to him. I'll need to take the lead. I'm kinda looking at Huntsville, all the space stuff, that sounds pretty exciting. I had a friend in school back home in Iowa who went to Space Camp. It's about the most exciting thing she's ever done. Hey, and she's part of NASA now."

"That's totally cool, run with your passion, your dream."

"That's what I've done, Lucas, my motto, save those I can. 'Course, God has a say in all that."

"Right, I've had to turn all my hopes and dreams over to Him. I'm kinda amazed how things've turned out."

"I take it you like what you do, at Auburn."

"Love it."

"I understand almost nothing about the whole technology deal, except when it comes to helping my patients get well."

"More and more'll help your sick ones, as time goes on, uh, the technology'll do that."

They descended the trail mostly in silence. Tyann enjoyed being outside with hearing the birds chirping and watching the wind beginning to shake the few leaves remaining on the trees.

They hugged after he walked her to her car at the trail head.

"We're so comfortable together; may I call you, to spend an evening with you?"

"I'd really like that."

∞

"What's happening for Thanksgiving?"

"Mom, the nicest family asked me to join them for the holiday and to bring a friend. I'm taking Lucas, my hiking buddy. Ben D., that's what he wants to be called, was a patient of mine during my first months as a visiting nurse. He lost his wife a year before that. What he needed was someone to lift him out of his funk. I did that. He could hardly walk with his walker. I encouraged him. He got better about walking in his home, switched to a cane of correct length, and we went for walks outside with his walker. He's so proud of his walks around the block, taking his cane, but only needing to use it occasionally. His daughter and son live away, but are coming for Thanksgiving. His housekeeper, Ben D. and I keep in touch; she's super and has the family's whole stay with Ben D. planned out. I'm really excited to meet them. They've heaped praise on me for helping their dad. Mom, all he needed was someone to encourage him to get up and continue to live his life. He goes to work out at a gym for older folks a couple times a week. And he's returned to church."

"Tyann, how wonderful; you would've never seen this end of his recovery had you been a nurse in a hospital. You're doing great work."

"What about you and dad?"

"Going to Mandy's, she's doing a turkey breast and the other good stuff. We're going to meet a man she's dated for a little while."

"Oh Mom, you'll keep me in the loop. I love you; hugs to dad."

"We love you, Tyann, Happy Thanksgiving."

Annie stood for a moment in the kitchen, looking out the window, at the snow beginning to swirl. Tears burned her eyes, as she spoke out in a strangled voice, "She did not say a single word about Conner. God bless and keep them both."

℘

She heard the doorbell ring.

"Glad I got ready; I'm so excited to hear the singers. Lucas says the music department, vocals, orchestra, just superb."

She peeked through the security peephole and stepped back, "Oh, no."

She opened the door and tried to smile.

"Hi Tyann, I wanted to stop by, to tell you I'll have a couple of hours."

Lucas appeared next to Conner.

He waved to her and angled his head toward Conner.

"Lucas, this is Conner."

"Conner, Lucas."

They shook hands. Tyann watched the enormous study in contrast, the tall and muscular doc-to-be and the much smaller and shorter IT guru with glasses.

"Yes, Lucas, I'm ready to go. Conner just dropped by for a sec."

"See ya Tyann; nice to meet you Lucas."

Conner could see by his suit and her stunning red dress and black coat that they headed out to an event.

"She looks so beautiful; you're an idiot, you should've called. She has her life, doofus," he told himself as he headed back to his car. He did not look back at the couple.

ଚ୍ଚ

Tyann took on a special nursing assignment through her visiting nurses group. The regular nurse needed to get away for two weeks over the holidays. Tyann subbed in. Many of her clients had special holiday plans of being away or being with family. Marjorie had a little while to live, inoperable brain cancer, in its last stages. She had her own bedroom and bath on the first floor, directly across from the library, where Tyann slept on a comfortable pull out couch, to be near her. Her doctor ordered a hospital bed when Majorie felt like she needed it. The time came, her husband's quandary, where to place the bed.

"I'm feeling more like myself this last couple of days. Nothing's been done for Christmas. It's a holiday time I love," Tyann remembered Marjorie's comment from the first day she took over the woman's care.

Tyann looked over the rest of the first floor, an open concept great room with a stone fireplace, dining area, and large kitchen.

"What about this; we'll put the tree here, your bed here, so you can watch all the activity going on."

"I like that, do it, I'm tired of being cooped up in a bedroom. I want to be out in a bed where the action is. And the half bath is close by. Christmas music, we have many CD's, I'd like to hear Christmas music all day long."

The hospital bed arrived the next day. And a 6 ½ ft. Douglas fir got delivered. Tyann worked with Howard to bring up boxes of Christmas decorations from storage. The rest of the decorations Marjorie requested he give to nonprofits

"We won't put up too much; she'll get tired quickly, but I'm sure she has favorites."

"She does, and, Tyann, you're marvelous, she's perked up so much since you've been here. She loves the holidays immensely. And we have grandchildren nearby. They're teenagers, absolutely devastated by what's happened to their meemaw. Oh, and I'm called their papaw. They're all going to be so pleased when they see her. And our son and daughter, too."

"I can take it from here, and Howard, to tell you." She turned to him and touched his shoulder, "take care of yourself. Your life's going on, after she's with God."

"I'm just glad it's the holidays, 'cause it's quieter in the law office, from the next little while."

"It'll give you a chance to breathe."

He smiled to her as they brought the boxes up.

"Hey Tyann, it's nice to do this."

"That's a really good thing; he's been so silent and emotionless, coping mechanism," she thought as she gazed at him.

By late that afternoon Marjorie saw the transformation of the Arlington home into a lovely Christmas scene. She even helped place the four stockings at the fireplace mantle, one stocking for each grandchild. She heard the Christmas music as she rested in what she called her "new" bed, right in the center of the room. She viewed the fireplace, tree, and into the dining area and kitchen. Marjorie rested as Tyann fixed her favorite meal, toasted cheese sandwiches with a bit of ketchup in the middle. She like the way Tyann did them, in a pan on the stove, cooked with butter.

The next day Marjorie asked Tyann to locate her address book. Together they prepared Christmas cards, one thing Marjorie did not think she would ever do again. Tyann addressed the cards.

"This is such a lovely peaceful scene," Marjorie touched the outside of the card, "with the snow, the deer and the mountains in the background. I knew one day I would use these cards. It's now."

"Would you like to say anything on the inside besides the Christmas wording?"

"Uh, you'll need to write."

"OK, dictate to me."

"Write   Take care and God bless and keep you all."

"Would you like to sign?"

"No, go ahead, my handwriting's too illegible now, you sign for me and Howard. And thanks for making a list of the people we send to, in case Howard wants to, another year."

About half way through the process Marjorie asked to lie down.

"Go ahead and finish up; I'd like them to go out tomorrow. Howard can take them and mail them from work."

The next morning Tyann heard her patient sobbing after she woke up.

"Tyann, I can't see out of my left eye, the doctor said that might happen, that I'd be blind before the cancer takes me. And I feel like I need more pain medication. It may be time to start the morphine."

Marjorie's doctor made a house call that afternoon.

Tyann's instructions remained simple, "Keep her comfortable."

After he left, both Marjorie's daughter and daughter-in-law stopped by to visit.

"Mom, everything looks so grand. Did Tyann help you with all this?"

"She did; she's a fabulous helper. And she's made chocolate chip bars and coffee for us. The bars just taste so great to me; you know I don't have much of an appetite."

The four women sat at the dining room table, with its festive red runner and poinsettia plant in the middle. They laughed and joked as the women shared their Christmas holiday happenings about their husbands and teen kids.

"You didn't want us here before; I'm glad you've decided to see us," her daughter-in-law said.

"Ladies, my pity party, it's over; each day I've got left is precious to me." She paused and smiled, looking at each one, including Tyann. "It just took me so long to see that. Please come over on Christmas day for afternoon snacks and goodies. All I have for the grandkids are gift certificates, but papaw knew which places they liked to shop at. So he took care of that."

"All we want, Marjorie, is to spend part of the day with you."

"Right, 'cause I tire easy."

Tyann heard the background music, the Mormon Tabernacle Choir singing Christmas carols.

Before they left, they asked to talk with Tyann in the library.

"Thank you for your very special care of mom. You even helped her get her Christmas cards out. And our growing-up home, it looks so grand. She's really perked up."

"She's asked me to tell you that she does not want you all here as time nears, only Howard, and me. Will you be OK with that? She says it's horrible to watch someone take their last breaths."

"Uh huh, that happened to her with both her parents. She's told us it almost kills the survivors, and the survivors are the ones who have to go on."

"So, as difficult as that sounds, that's the way she wants it. Marjorie wants her children and grandchildren to remember all the good times you all have had together."

"How wonderful of her; the way she is and has always been," her daughter, Ellie, smiled as Tyann watched tears start. They both hugged Tyann and stopped at the easy chair where their mom sat, near her bed.

"We'll see you Christmas afternoon, Meemaw. And the four grand'uns, they'll stop by as they can, kinda unannounced."

"Perfect, I'll just be resting or up and about. They're welcome anytime during the day. My nights are hardest, the pain."

After they hugged, the ladies exited the home Ellie grew up in.

"Wow, Ellie, it was so good to see your mom."

"Whew Jo, it went much better than I had expected. But the doctor said that mom might bounce back, especially for the holidays. And then she'll maybe let go."

The two women hugged and then walked to their separate cars.

"Gosh, mom even made sure a Christmas wreath got hung by the front door where she always wants it," Ellie spoke out as she looked at the front area, before she got in her car.

℘

Marjorie took communion along with Tyann on Christmas morning. One of the family's parish priests stopped by, a special request from the family for her. That afternoon Ellie and Donovan stopped by with their spouses and kids. Howard lit the gas log fireplace and played the Christmas CD's as the family gathered around meemaw's bed.

"Last night, oh wondrous, a group of singers from one of my organizations dropped by and sang Christmas carols to me, Howard and Tyann. I so wanted to hear a group in person."

They clapped tor her as they murmured how nice that was, to do on Christmas Eve. They helped themselves to egg nog, wassail, and Christmas cookies, fudge and divinity. Marjorie handed each grandchild a gift certificate in an envelope.

Thank you, Meemaw," they spoke in unison. They knelt near her as they sang *Silent Night.* Howard and all the other adults joined in.

Marjorie clapped after they finished, "I love you all; thank you."

After the families left, she gave a weak smile, "I'm really happy, so special to be with the family; I'm so glad I told them."

Tyann spoke to Howard,. "Marjorie must rest now. Because she ate very little and drank less, the doctor's put her on an IV saline drop. Now I give her morphine via the drip."

Once Marjorie slept Howard asked Tyann to track what his wife asked him to do as she knew the end was not far away.

"She said to me, 'Howard, I'm going to God. Let's not put the kids through this agony of deciding what's what.'"

"What did that mean for her?"

"Well, she said it'd probably be Christmas, so we've done what she wanted, to be together for this day, a happy Christmas time. She explained that the horror was going through her stuff: clothes, jewelry, makeup, shoes, everything. We did that together, just the two of us, and it's all inventoried, boxed up and ready for the nonprofits. The furniture we no longer wanted, and many household goods I did not want to move with me, already've been taken away. She's made it simpler for me. Oh, she's kept a very few things back, for the kids and grandkids, but only if they want the stuff. They won't have to make a lot of decisions, 'cause there's not much stuff."

"She's done a masterful job, with your help. 'Course, don't you do estate situations yourself?"

"I do, that's what's made all this understandable for me. Except for this one's got a lot of emotion. But her will, life insurance, her retirement stuff, all in order, her car's been sold."

"Uh, you mentioned about moving , are you planning to sell this home and move?"

"Yes, to a much smaller place, this house is ready to sell; I'll wait 'til spring, when it'll have a better chance of selling."

"Marjorie helped you with that?"

"Right, from the time of her first diagnosis, she's helped; she wanted to do it. There's no pity party for her. Since I've gotten into estate planning, I've shared lots of death and dying scenarios with her."

"So she understands, and she's a fighter, to make it to Christmas."

They moved out into the hall, away from the master bedroom and spoke in quiet voices.

"I'll move into a smaller bedroom, until I sell. You know, the memories."

"Telling you, Howard, as I tell all my patient families in situations like yours, you absolutely must take care of yourself, plenty of fluids, eat wholesome food, exercise, watch the alcohol, go to grief counseling. You've been married a long time, and the grieving is a long process."

"Yeah, I know 'cause I'm already feeling the loss of her; the shadow downstairs is not who I knew."

"Right, I need to go check on her. Then we can talk in the basement; you have more to say and it's where you've got things stored."

Fifteen minutes later Tyann met him in the basement. He paced back and forth, restless, she could see.

"Am I handling this OK, do you think, Tyann?"

"You are, and admirably, I might add."

"Uh, what's your situation, when she's gone?"

"Let's sit down."

They each found a box to sit on.

"My duties end once I'm cleared by the authorities. Contact the medical supply store to have them come and take the hospital bed away. You may want to keep the Christmas decorations up. And for New Year's I strongly advise you to gather your family for a private family celebration, just you and your two kids and families. From what Marjorie tells me, there's no funeral, just her ashes for the family to deal with, and a celebration of her life, very soon after she goes to God. She's even got the caterer picked out. And Ellie has a list of people to contact. I mean, Marjorie's got it all taken care of."

"As she always has, a master organizer."

"Talk to her, Howard, this may be your last opportunity."

"I'll go now and do that."

"I'll give you two some privacy; going out for a short walk.

⁊

Before she went to sleep that Christmas night, she asked Tyann to take away the IV drip, to just give her only a little morphine because she felt completely doped up.

"Come close, Tyann, I've been talking to God. He says it's time to tell you what an awesome job you've done taking care of me, of Howard, and helping with my family. God bless and keep you, and my family."

Marjorie slept after 8 p.m. that evening. Tyann felt completely wrung out, like a tiresome old mop, as she stepped away from the woman's bed. The doorbell rang. She peeked out and felt her breath coming hard, feeling weak, like she might faint. She opened the door with some difficulty.

"Conner."

She motioned with her finger on her lips that they needed to be quiet.

"Tyann," he whispered, "can I come in? I called your folks and they told me about your special duty nursing, where you were. I didn't want to call this home, not to disturb. But I needed to see you."

"Of course, come in."

She looked up to him and saw tears.

"Let's go into the library; my patient's sleeping."

She continued to speak in a quiet tone to him as they sat down on the couch.

"I think she'll go to God, tonight or early morning."

"Tyann, pops had an MI on the 23rd."

"How bad?"

"Serious, some blockage, maybe bypass, not sure."

"Done with your unit?"

"Just finished, I get a four-day break, and then back at it. So I'm flying home to do my own assessment, to be with them."

She saw the tears stream down his cheeks. She let him cry, just took his hand and held it.

"Brenden didn't smoke, just gained some weight, but he's gotta turn things over to helpers."

"I think he gets that now."

"I'll keep all the Mulrenan family in my prayers, thoughts."

"It's getting better for me, Tyann. I'm going to make it, to get through all the units. I had a terrible, rough start. My studying's coming along for the accreditation exam. Maybe we could see each other once in a while."

"That's up to you, Conner, ball's in your court."

"I know, uh tell me what're your thoughts, about us."

"I have to go check on Marjorie. I'll be right back, but you'll need to go in a few minutes."

Tyann looked down at Marjorie and saw her smile. Her patient turned her head first to the fireplace and then to the tree. Tyann watched her nod her head and smile again. She lifted her hand as if to wave to Tyann and then drifted back to sleep.

She stepped back into the library. Conner saw the serious look in her eyes and her thin lips.

"It'd be nice to see you again. This special duty really helped me financially. But I'll be back to my visiting nurse rotation, starting on Sunday. I've decided I'm going to Huntsville. I want to be with the engineers, the space folks. I had a chance to go look at apartments. Plus, I had interviews at several hospitals in the area. They're impressed with my background, my trauma work. They're sadly short on nurses with the critical care background, especially younger nurses. I've had two offers.

Some of the older folks really need to get out of the nursing field; it's stress-driven and many of them carry too much weight and have heart and diabetes problems of their own. And the hours, still pretty terrible, some still have that 12-hour crazy shift."

"Wow, Tyann, you're on top of it. I'll go now."

"Please let me know how your poppa's getting along, and say hello to your momma. All my life, your poppa and momma, well they're awesome; you're lucky to have them for parents."

She watched him give her an unsmiling nod.

"I've got your number; I'll leave you a message."

"Let yourself out; I've got to check on Marjorie."

Howard came down after he showered. He planned to sit with his wife through the night, so he dressed in comfortable sweats, slippers, and his favorite Auburn sweatshirt.

He pulled her special recliner next to the bed.

"Tyann, I'll keep the gas log on, keep the home fires burning, and the Christmas tree lit, in case she wakes up. You go to bed; I'll call you if I need to, hear?"

She saw the understanding smile and a tiny shine in his dark eyes. She nodded to him and went to her bed in the library with the door open, so she could hear sounds nearby. She wore her pink comfy sweats and let her hair down her back. They settled down at 11 and Tyann checked on them at 2. Howard leaned into her bed and held Marjorie's hand. They both slept. She checked again at 5. Howard lay in bed with Marjorie. He turned to his side laying his arm across his wife.

"She's with our God in heaven," Tyann whispered.

She let him sleep until 6 and gently roused him.

"Thank you Tyann, I was so glad to be with her when she went to her next home."

She called the proper authorities and then made coffee for them both. They sat, drinking the strong brew.

"I'll stay, until the authorities arrive and decide how you want to handle everything. Then I need to leave you, to go on. You're gonna do fine; just give it time. Remember that it'll hit you when you least expect it. You're in shock," she paused, "now."

Howard put on a jacket and proper shoes and left the house for a short walk to clear his head. He returned as Tyann finished packing up her belongings and making up the sleeping couch. He insisted he would take care of the sheets later. She went to the kitchen for a second cup of coffee and donuts she brought for them several days ago. They stood across the kitchen island from each other as they talked and ate.

"They'll be here any minute. And Tyann, I want you to have this. Marjorie, well she was all about giving. She hinted that you're a minimalist, so down the road, that you had a fella you struggled with, an almost completed DVM student here. I hope and pray everything will turn out OK."

"God's will, sir," she opened the envelope, "oh my goodness, thank you."

She smiled to him, her first smile in some time.

He looked at her, "She's gonna light up some guy's life, one day," he thought.

Then he said, "No, thank you, you made her last days as positively marvelous as they could be, going on, day by day, she knew the day she was in, how precious it was."

They heard the doorbell ring. Tyann stayed until the authorities indicated she had handled everything they needed. Howard came to her, kissed her on the cheek, and hugged her. As she turned at the front door, he waved to her and smiled.

∽

"I'm not sure I can take another step, but I need to stop by my church and talk to God."

Tyann did that.

"I feel better now," she said as she walked down the steps from the church.

She headed home to her tiny apartment. She showered and slept for many hours. When she woke up, she showered again and made herself an egg, bacon, and toast breakfast.

"How'd it go, Tyann?"

"She died, early the morning after Christmas Day, Dad, as we expected. I'm glad I had the experience. She was brave, so understanding of what her family needed, so much the mom, to the end. It's been a grand lesson for me."

"We have guests for dinner, Sarah and Conner Mulrenan; did you know he flew home?"

"Yeah, he stopped by at my patient's home, and told me Christmas night."

"I'm glad he talked to you; a while since you've seen him."

"Yup, he's on a break for four days, before his next unit. He's feeling more positive about the rest of his term."

"Your mom and I stopped by to see Brenden last evening at Porttown Memorial. He's got to make some lifestyle changes."

"Right, hope you and mom are takin' care of yourselves." She giggled, "You got nurses surrounding you, mom, and me."

"Uh huh, I gotta behave; actually I'm doing good, lost some weight, and I'm goin' to a gym twice a week, can you imagine that?"

"Good for you, Dad, keep it up. Brenden's poppa'll need to do some cardio rehab, once they figure out what to do about his situation. Hey, say hi to Sarah and Conner for me, oh and also if you see Brenden. And I got a lot of decisions to make, on my own."

"I know you have; I'll pass along your greetings, hugs, love you my Tyann."

"Hugs to mom, love you, Dad."

7

1997 – Huntsville, Alabama

"Decisions made, here I am, standing in the ER, back where I belong."

Tyann acknowledged her decisions. She got offered the position she wanted, in the hospital she wanted. As she ended her shift that Saturday afternoon in early May, she pondered one question.

"Do I return to Auburn, or do I stay here in Huntsville?"

Several male nurses and one doctor already expressed a personal interest in her. The one thing they all shared with her concerned the critical care experience she already possessed, as a fairly new nurse. The other item became her ability to make do with whatever materials she had, at hand. In Punta Cana she devised several apparatuses and one procedure that helped patients get through incision healing quicker. Those patient improvements impressed this hospital crew.

One nurse asked her out after coffees together at the outside hospital patio. The date coincided with a graduation. She decided to tell the honest truth, that she felt torn about seeing the graduate again, as opposed to starting a new dating scenario.

"He's been a part of your life for a very long time; weren't you dating uh, didn't you say you dated his older brother, who died, right?"

"That's correct, Jeff; for eight years we've been friends, oh gosh, before that, back to grade school. I do love him."

She watched Jeff's smile to her and she heard the tone of his voice, sincere.

"Definitely you should go to his ceremony; the DVM is a really big deal. He's gonna heal animals, just like we're healing humans. And you guys, well you grew up together, like you said, it'll maybe help you figure out what you want. Hey, you clearly don't know exactly what you want in a love relationship, isn't that right?"

"Yeah, you're right on about that. Thanks, Jeff, I need to see him, celebrate his achievement, and get to know him again."

"Sounds like there're eight years of catchin' up to do."

"There are."

∞

Tyann rented a car at the Montgomery airport and drove to Auburn. She planned to stay at Ben D.'s home. He wanted to see her, and he asked if he could go to Conner's DVM ceremony with her.

His housekeeper greeted her and helped her to her room.

"He's at the gym; he's anxious to see you. You were a miracle worker for him."

"I'm glad, Celestina; you've been a loyal helper and companion to him. I hope you'll continue with him."

"Of course, Miss Tyann, this really is my home; I just have a place to sleep and spend weekends. I get to see my grandkids as much as I want. Ben compensates me handsomely. I've put money away for my retirement, but that won't be for a long time."

Tyann and Ben D. went for a hike the next morning.

"It's good to be back on my hiking trail, and Ben D., you're doing so good. We need to get back to get ready for the ceremony."

"Does he know you're here?"

They descended, with Ben leading, using the thick walking stick Tyann suggested he use.

"I told him I wasn't sure I'd be able to switch with several other nurses who'd work my shift for me. But I was able to swing it. When I graduated from IU he surprised me by coming to my nursing graduation."

Ben D. laughed, "So you're sorta returning the favor."

"Right."

80

She felt tears welling up in her eyes as she heard his name called. Conner strode across the stage, shook hands and touched his diploma to his heart. She turned to Ben D. He nodded and smiled to her. She smiled back through her tears.

"I didn't recognize him, with that cap and gown on. He seems bigger than I remember."

After ceremony Tyann tried to follow his movements. He definitely stood head and shoulders over most of the other graduates. And then she saw them, his poppa and momma, greeting him. Tyann held Ben D.'s hand, guiding him to where they stood among the crowd of happy graduates and families.

Conner saw her, a small beautiful blonde in a pretty spring dress, holding the hand of an older gentleman.

Ben D. let go of her hand so she could greet the new doctor. She stepped forward as Sarah and Brenden moved back from their son.

Conner held out his arms to Tyann. They came together in a quiet hug.

"Oh, Tyann, you came, man, what a surprise!"

She stepped back from his hug and laughed, "Remember, doc, you did the same thing to me, came to my graduation unannounced."

Then she saw it, that light in his eyes, that had not been there for some time. She hugged Sarah and then Brenden. She gave him her nurse's look, as she eyed him from head to toe.

"Uh, do I pass inspection?"

She heard the humor in his voice.

"I dunno; have to get the true skinny from Sarah."

Everyone laughed.

"Sorry, Mulrenan's, this is my friend, Ben D."

They all shook hands with him.

"Yes, I was one of her patients, when she did her visiting nurse stint here in Auburn. She basically resurrected me from the dead. And she kept checking on me after I left her care. We've become friends. She talked about all of you, especially on our walks; she got me out walking, with a walker, then a cane, now, look at me."

"Sir, you're doing well," Conner commented as he smiled to Ben D. "Let's find a place at the reception area, to sit down and chat. When the line thins down, we'll get cake and punch."

Early that evening Conner met Tyann at Ben D.'s. It cooled down, so they went for a walk.

"What now, Tyann?"

"I'm so happy for you. And for us, I don't know. Share your plan. I fly out in the morning, thank goodness, it's just a short hop; will be working several double shifts to pay back the nurses who covered for me."

He took her hand and held it as they walked along.

"I can't practice until I get accredited; I passed exams, but the accrediting process takes time. So my plan, I'll vet tech in a practice in Decatur, and start looking for a practice to join as soon as I'm the real thing."

"Gosh, Decatur's on the outskirts of Huntsville."

"Yeah, I know, I want to get to know you again, Tyann. It's been a long haul; we've changed so much in these last years."

"Do you eventually want your own practice?"

"Maybe, but I gotta work through that DVM debt. And buying a practice, even a partnership is gonna be so pricey. The debt's driving me crazy already. And vet tech's don't make much, so I'll continue to struggle."

"But it's not with school, taking classes."

"Uh huh, my mind's a lot clearer, now that I think I know where I'm headed."

"And I want to get to know you, Conner. Time's changed us a lot. Your poppa looks good, lost the weight he should."

"I've kept up with momma on his cardio rehab. He goes twice a week and is getting a lot stronger."

"You got a place?"

"Yeah, a little one bedroom, in Decatur, not that far from the vet clinic."

"I'm lucky, working days, four 10 hours, Monday-Wednesday, and Saturdays. Nurses never seem to get a full weekend off."

"Do you like it?"

"Yeah, ER, critical care, I've already done one helicopter airlift, our patient survived and thrived."

"Your experience in Punta Cana?"

"Absolutely the best thing I could've ever done. Talk about improvising, the water and hospital bacteria situation there. At this hospital they call me the bleach lady. I brought all I learned back here. Our hospital had to do some cleanup too. There're new bugs out there that defy antibiotics. All we can do is try to keep the place as bacteria free as possible."

"You know that's impossible," he paused, "yeah, I know, you gotta try."

He squeezed her hand and let go as they neared Ben D.'s home.

"May I call you once I get settled in Decatur?"

"I'd like that, send me an e-mail, if you get that. But please, settle in, feet on the ground first, lots ahead."

"I will."

They hugged as they stood by the front door.

She looked up to him and saw the special light in his eyes, "Congratulations again, be safe, God bless and keep you, Conner."

"God keep you too, uh, He blesses you, Tyann."

℘

Jeffrey and Tyann finally got a chance to chat two weeks after she returned to the Huntsville Med Center ER. On break they sat in a corner of the hospital's basement cafeteria.

"So?"

"Yeah, Jeffrey, I'm gonna try again with him. He's moved to Decatur, doing vet tech work until his accreditation comes through, takes time. I haven't seen him yet since his move; his phone message just mentioned so far, so good."

"I'll just be your friend, then, Tyann. You need space."

"Jeffrey, date others; lots of ladies out there, in this super smart biotech community."

"I haven't met many, yet."

"U. of Alabama, Huntsville, checked that place out?"

"That's an idea; most ladies look at me kinda wonky when I tell them I'm a nurse."

"Well, they don't comprehend medical; male nurses are gonna grow in numbers; we need you guys, just like we've got female docs. Do they know about the good money you make?"

"Nope, never've gotten that far along in a relationship to get asked that. Most super materialistic ones first wanta know what kind of car I drive."

"Uh, let's see, your little 1989 brownish pickup, right?"

He nodded to her.

"Dude," she gazed at him for a minute, then shook her head, "if that turns them off, well, that's not the kind of lady you want on your arm, anyway."

"Right, want somebody like you, comfortable on a trail, or appreciative of the music at a concert, yeah, like stuff we've done together."

"Hey, bub, I'm your trial run," she laughed.

He touched her shoulder and just shook his head.

"Let's get outa here."

ജ

Late September breezes cooled the humid Huntsville area. The drier days, without so much rain, agreed with everyone. Tyann followed Conner up the rocky trail in the Chapman mountains outside Huntsville.   She enjoyed the wind caressing her face as they got to the top.

"Going to church with you today, that was great. I was so lucky to not have to go in, no critter in surgery recovery that needed to stay overnight.   And, now, being out here with you. This is what you do many Sundays?"

"Uh huh, early church, then head up here. I used to come up earlier, right after church, because of the heat. But this is not quite like Punta Cana; it seemed more humid there than here, well, beachy.   And my place, we just had fans, air conditioning, wow, I still consider it a luxury."

"Well, folks here wouldn't survive if they didn't have it. I can't even imagine the old days, before electricity, and they wore more clothes."

"Folks just adjust; humans're that way."

They took a few minutes to look around, a full 360 view of the area.

"Glorious sights," he nodded to her, "sit?"

"Yeah, I need to; yesterday, busy shift, in the afternoon. Glad the ER is compact, not too much walking, but it's pretty old. They're talking about a newly constructed place for us, maybe in a couple years."

They drank water and helped themselves to trail mix she packed for both of them.

He turned to her, "I've heard back."

"Oh, Conner, tell me."

He heard the excitement in her voice as she smiled to him. I'm a doc, for reals."

They hugged, a long strong hug. She raised her lips to his. He caressed her lips, touched his tongue to her tongue. They kissed and kissed.

He put his arm around her shoulder, "Wonderful, your kiss."

She squeezed his hand.

Her mind danced ahead, as they worked their way down the rocky trail.

"Back off, Tyann, one day at a time," she whispered as she descended.

He drove them back to her place and walked her to her door.

He looked down to her, "I've big decisions; we've big decisions."

"Time," she spoke as she smiled up to him.

He nodded and took her in his arms, hugging her and swinging her around in a circle. He set her down. She felt his kiss on the top of her head.

"Like in the old days," she told herself.

She watched him return to his car and wave to her. She waved back.

હ૭

"I'm so happy you're here; this is my first place you two've seen."

Annie smiled to her, "It's perfect for you; certain you've got everything you need?"

"Yeah, Mom, thanks, remember minimalist me. When I helped dad bring in stuff, I noticed you guys drove a pickup here. It's got Iowa plates."

"Conner didn't tell you?" her dad asked.

"Nope."

"He and his dad're trading vehicles. Conner's getting Brenden's three-year-old pickup; it's a good size for him, you know, vets go out and about the country, to farms, ranches, wherever there're critters that need medical care. It's already got a nice stainless steel storage area in the open back end, something he'll need for his medical supplies. We're driving Conner's car back to Porttown."

"Wow, that's really nice of you two to do that."

"A neighborly gesture, since we planned to visit you over Christmas, Brenden gave us money for gas both ways. Driving's cheaper than plane fare, and the bummer hassle at airports."

"Making the vehicle exchange?"

"Tomorrow, I told Brenden I'd help Conner get the Alabama emissions done plus do the title exchange, and new Alabama plates. Brenden gave me cash to help with that transaction. It'll be pricey for plates 'cause it's newer, and pickups have lots of value. Conner'll have to take care of the change of vehicle on his insurance."

"So, oh yeah, all the same stuff'll be done to Conner's car when it gets back to Iowa."

"Right, just gotta make sure Conner signs his car's title over, and that we take the title with us to give to Brenden."

"Gotcha, what a super cool Christmas present for Conner; he'll be here as soon as he closes the clinic. The doc gives him almost complete responsibility, like it's his clinic already."

"Wow, that's a super level of trust in Conner."

"From what he says, most times the clinic runs like a fine machine."

"That's very lucky for Conner."

"Hey, how's your car runnin?"

"Dad, I plan to keep it for two more years, unless it starts needing too much time and money fixin' it up. I'm making good money now, but that wasn't the case overseas and doing the visiting nurse stuff. I really gotta look at my future, socking money away, from right now on."

"Very smart."

℘

"What is that awesome smell?"

"Check the oven, big guy."

Conner open the oven door, "Ah, ham, smells like you added some syrup."

"I did. We'll be ready to eat in a little while. You and dad are in charge of getting the table ready. Mom's got her assigned task of fixing the salad. I just need to pop in the rolls."

"Poker after?" Tyrone asked.

"Course."

As they sat down to pumpkin pie and whipped topping, Tyann poured coffee for all of them.

"Still I'm an old fashioned kinda guy, so Tyrone and Annie, I'm requesting your permission to marry Tyann."

She held Conner's hand and nodded to her parents, "I said yes."

Tyrone looked at Annie. She nodded her head.

"Yes, we give our permission. And after all this time, we were never sure."

"Pop's heart attack, that was the tipping point for me. None of us know how many days God's gonna give us."

They all nodded to Conner.

"And Tyann, you see how precious life is, you see breath go out of people's lives, all the time in your work," Annie added.

"We've spent as much time together as we can the last three months. We've talked with our priest, will be going to pre-nuptial counseling, 'cause for us, we've struggled for a time in our relationship."

Conner touched Tyann's shoulder, "Had to get reacquainted all over again. We sure aren't the same people we were eight years ago, when we each went our separate ways, to IU and ISU."

"It's been, well, very special to observe each other, how we've turned out," Tyann smiled to Conner, "so far. We'll share plans, and Conner has news."

"Right, so, after the first of the year I'll help in a clinic on the eastern edge of Huntsville; helping with large animals on the surrounding farms and ranches. I like the vet in charge; he's lost his partner who's had to give up the work because of a rheumatoid arthritis condition. If all goes well, I'll hopefully buy in as a partner in a few years.

You all know I have a mountain of debt to pay back. I'll not burden Tyann with that. I'm insisting she sock as much money away as she can into her hospital-sponsored 401K. Oh, I'll be well compensated for the work I'll be doing."

"What about you, Tyann?"

"I'm excited for us; I plan to stay on at my med center; I love the work. At some point, I'll leave trauma care, and do less stressful nursing. But for now, it's what I want, my reason for being."

"Coming home to get married?"

"We are," Conner smiled to Tyrone and Annie.

"By a stream."

"Tell us more."

Tyann turned to Conner and nodded.

"We have a favorite place on the Mulrenan farm, like Tyann says, by a stream, where we've picnicked and looked up at the night stars. Just family, and whichever priest who can help us. We've asked pops and momma, they've said yes to a reception for more folks, at the farm house. Seems like a thousand years ago that we were together for our high school graduation. We just don't know many folks back there anymore. So the reception's kinda for my parents and you two. Your friends and theirs will be invited."

"We think, a Saturday in June, when we both can get away for four days."

"It'll have to be our honeymoon coming to Iowa and heading back here to Alabama."

"What a happy Christmas for us," Annie gazed at them and her husband and nodded, "your glorious news."

&

The emergency department stayed quiet on Tyann's shift, that is, until 11:00 a.m. It seemed that's when folks realized how sick they were. The ambulances started bringing folks in. Tyann called it the 11 o'clock wave. But today was harder, since it was Christmas Eve, when folks wanted to be with loved ones.

Annie took Tyann to work so she could have a car for shopping. Tyrone and Conner spent a good part of the day getting the pickup fixed up for driving in Alabama.

They stood in the parking lot of Conner's apartment. Conner had two screwdrivers in hand.

"I didn't know whether the screws would be phillips or regular."

He knelt on one knee as he replaced the Iowa plates with the new Alabama plates

"Unbelievable, just unbelievable, the cost of plates on a newer vehicle. Is it like that in Iowa?"

"Oh yeah."

"Now I really appreciate my older wheels, and the small license plate fee."

"And lower cost of your car insurance, your dad mentioned to remind you of taking care of that, calling your insurance agent. Take a deep breath after he tells you the new cost, plus you'll use the pickup as part of your vet business, getting around to the critters."

"Thank you again, Tyrone, for your assistance with all this, all the little details of changing cars. All my life you folks have helped our family. You're great neighbors, especially that first fall corn harvest after Brody died. My folks, absolutely devastated, you helped organize the harvesting."

Tyrone smiled to Conner, "Yup, we got're done." He paused, "And the Mulrenan family's always been there for us, so cool that we'll all go on together, you marrying Tyann."

ಐ

"We're taking you out to early dinner and then present opening. Is Conner meeting us for midnight mass?"

"He wasn't sure."

"We have to leave early tomorrow morning, Tyann."

"I know, you have to get back to the shop and to the nursing facility."

"Pretty much, we'll not see you again until the ceremony in June."

"Right."

Candle lighting at midnight mass instilled a breathlessness in Tyann, the darkened church and the light-studded trees at the sides of the altar.

"My whole life, singing *Silent Night* with my family, and now with Conner included, kinda the ultimate of my religious experience," she thought and nodded to herself.

In the parking lot after mass Conner hugged Annie and Tyrone.

"Safe travels back, and give my folks a hug for me, OK?"

"Will do, and Merry Christmas to you both," he nodded to Conner and to Tyann. "'Course we'll see Tyann until morning. And good luck, Conner with your new practice."

Conner nodded to them, waved, and headed for his pickup.

On the way to her apartment Annie asked her daughter, "You're seeing him over the holidays?"

"Yes, some, I'm doing some covering for several married nurses, to give them a chance to be with their families between now and the day after New Year's."

"How many days're you working?"

"Eight straight, but that's OK, cause I'll need them to do the same for me in June. It'll take a while to build up my annual leave at the hospital."

ဆ

Jeffrey met her on break when they both returned to the ER after holidays.

"I been watchin' you, smiling girl. You must have news for me."

"Perceptive dude, you're that, uh huh, he asked, and I accepted."

Jeff watched her smile to him widen.

"You're a happy girl, soon?"

"June."

"Hey, congratulations, uh, we're not gonna lose you?"

"No way, I'm here, love it, as long as I got cool dudes like you to work with."

He picked up her left hand, "No engagement ring?"

"Nope, just want a diamond in the middle of a wide band."

"Getting married back home?"

"Yeah, our ties, our families're back there. We don't know many folks here, with our crazy, well, medical schedules. It's gonna take a while."

"I'm seeing a woman, some; maybe one day we can double date. You'll like her, and I wanna meet your doc."

ဆ

"I believe you two will be ready."

"Think so, Father?"

"Yes, you've completed your prenup work. It's important now that you continue to get to know each other. Mostly apart for eight years, that's a long time, but I know it'll be hard for you, given your difficult and conflicting schedules. I so admire medical folks."

"Uh huh, we must take advantage of the little time we have together."

"It's still going to be?"

"Early June, before it gets crazy hot and humid in corn land."

Father laughed at Tyann's name for her area.

"And you've got a priest who'll help?"

"We do."

They stood together in Father's Huntsville rectory office and held hands. Father spoke a prayer for them, for their upcoming marriage.

"Please come home with me tonight."

Tyann smiled up to him, "I'll follow you; I've stuff to do in the morning."

He let her in and held her close.

"Remember what you asked me to do, the OBGYN?"

"Uh huh," then it hit him, "oh my goodness, on the pill."

"Yeah, for a month, seem to be doing just fine."

They took their coats off and began to undress each other in his living room. He picked her up and carried her to his bedroom.

"My love, oh my love," he crooned to her as he covered her face and neck with kisses. She returned his kisses with hers, moving down his chest, to his belly, and then kissing his throbbing penis. He pulled her up to him and took first one nipple and then the other into his mouth, gently sucking each one.

"Conner, Conner," she whispered as enormous heat suffused her groin, moving up her breasts to her head. He moved above her and entered her. They thrust into each other, again and again until they exploded together, riding their orgasms. Conner stayed with her, until their breathing calmed. He lifted from her and they lay together side by side, kissing and caressing each other's bodies. They came together again, this time, in the quiet of their more satisfied bodies.

"Wow."

"Yes wow."

They clung to each other. Later they fell into an exhausted sleep.

She roused, and turned to him. He lay on his side, watching her as she wakened.

"How long you been watching me?"

"Little while; know you have to get to your place, stuff you're doing."

"I love you, Conner."

"I love you, Tyann. You're the sun of my mornings and the fire of my nights. Do you remember me telling you that, years ago?"

"I do, at an evening picnic, you and me, near where we'll be married."

The next morning Conner padded around in his kitchen in stocking feet. He wore his favorite ISU sweatshirt and raggedy sweats. She came up behind him and put her arms around his chest.

"Thank you for making coffee. I'll have some and then get to my place."

He turned and came into a hug with Tyann. They looked into each other's eyes.

"Hhhmmm, that love light's in your eyes."

"Lemesee," she looked up into his dark blue eyes, "Yup, love light's there, in your eyes too."

They laughed together and hugged again.

℘

"There was a bad storm, guys. The area where you want to have the ceremony, it got pretty messed up," Mandy told them as Conner and Tyann arrived at the family home outside Porttown the day before the wedding.

"Not to worry, we got this handled. Uh, what about everything else?"

"Reception's covered by caterers who'll stay and clean up, per your instructions; you guys made it so easy for us."

"Good, we'll change and head over to my folks for gear we need."

Tyann and Conner helped Mandy. They raked and cut up branches that got stripped from the trees in the windstorm. They got the area cleaned up in a couple of hours. Tyann decided on how long and wide a path she wanted to walk with her dad to meet the priest and Conner. The three of them made a boundary of blown-down small pieces of wood on either side of the path.

"Yeah, I like the way everything looks. We'll all just stand for maybe 10 minutes. Hey, this's fun, haven't had a chance to be outside for that long."

Conner added, "In quite a while. We're kept inside, well you are. I'm really loving being able to travel around a bit."

"Yeah, that's a favorite remembrance of visiting nursing."

℘

"Father, ready for us?"

"I am," Father Mercer nodded, "I think the sky will hold for a bit."

Both Conner and Father looked up to see gray clouds scamper across the sun. Mandy stood on the bride's side and Brenden stood on the groom's. They consented to be witnesses for the ceremony. Conner watched Tyann walk up the path, her hand crooked in her dad's arm. She looked ahead, giving him her wide smile.

"It's a beautiful white dress for you, my bride and daisies in your hair, awesome," Conner whispered.

Conner and Tyann spoke of compass north, how each guided the other through the tumult of eight years, heading toward where they both wanted to be, their true north. Father took over. And the sky held.

The cake and champagne reception at the Mulrenan's celebrated Tyann and Conner. They got reacquainted with folks they had not seen since leaving for college. And they specifically requested no gifts. The reception invitation indicated a donation be sent to a Shriner's Children's Hospital to honor the couple if the invited guests wanted to participate somehow.

After that they returned to Alabama and moved to a two bedroom place between where each of them worked. It took a month, again because of their schedules.

"I'm moved in, but I have so little stuff," Tyann told Conner as they decided where to put his belongings.

"So glad I got a queen bed. It'll be perfect for us. I kinda thought it was sorta big, just for me."

"Doc, you were just thinkin' ahead, and you did not know it."

He smiled to her and gathered her in his arms.

୫୬

"Hey, whatcha doin' for the next couple hours?"

"Just boring house stuff; dinner'll be easy."

"Can you meet me at the clinic; I'd like you to see something."

"I'm on my way."

Conner drove them to a ranch five miles outside Huntsville.

"I spent a bit of time here in the last few weeks. Want ya to see."

Conner led Tyann to a corral where a big and beautiful chocolate mare stood.

"Check the little guy out."

Tyann stood on the fence and looked over to a far side of the area. She saw him, a brown and white, very small colt.

"We almost lost him, at birth. And then he picked up a bad infection, somehow cut his right front leg."

"Was it one of those super bugs, like people are getting, resistant to antibiotics?"

"Pretty much, it took a combination of two different medicines to get him well."

The little colt made a slow walk toward Conner.

"Yeah, he knows me; I think he somehow can tell that I helped make him well."

Conner reached through the wood fence and gave the colt a gentle pat on his forehead.

"Whatcha think?"

She looked up to him, "That you love what you do, that you enjoy helping animals."

"Right on."

"And I help folks."

"Yeah, you do," he looked to her and smiled.

"We love our work, and we love each other."

They kissed and held on tight.

The Irish situation for the Mulrenan and other families: In 1994 military activities in Northern Ireland slowed and some years later the Good Friday agreement occurred. In 2009 military groups in the areas were decommissioned.

A SCARF OF PROMISE

Sixteen-year-old Kaylee loves Rob. She becomes a widow. While driving to a medical meeting in a distant town she eyewitnesses an accident. Kyle is a second responder and assists Kaylee in removing a teen from his wrecked vehicle. Kyle is awed by Kaylee's bravery, looks, and competence. He loves her, upon first sight. They introduce themselves to each other by first name. Kyle searches for Kaylee for several years.

Kaylee knits a scarf her church group sends along with supplies and goodies for American soldiers in Afghanistan. The scarf travels back to a soldier's home in a trunk. The scarf brings Kyle and Kaylee together. Despite difficult circumstances Kaylee falls in love with Kyle. They marry. Kaylee moves her sons to Kyle's home in a different community. The family adjusts and love grows between Kaylee and Kyle. She accepts a nursing position, and another child comes to their family. The scarf of promise continues to bring love, this time to family close to Kaylee and Kyle.

ABOUT CATHLEEN

WWW.CATHLEENELLIS.COM

Cathleen Ellis is a Colorado native. She and her husband, John, live in the northern part of the state. They have four sons, three daughters-in-law, and four grandchildren. Cathleen draws the inspiration for her love stories from the lives of young people with whom she has lived and worked her entire life.